KV-747-472

The Man From Abilene

In the aftermath of the Civil War, renegade army officers fell into a way of life that was ideal for outlaws. Cold, hard and vicious, they set up laws of their own, governed wide stretches of territory and brought in the frock-coated gamblers to run their saloons for them.

Before long, however, the very lawlessness of these men forced Texas to take action. It needed a strong-minded man to go into these outlaw strongholds, a man who knew that he would live only so long as he could outdraw his enemies. Such a man was Bart Nolan, United States Marshal, a man who could not hide behind the star of his profession until he had obtained all of the evidence he needed.

Here was a man determined to kill to prevent these vicious killers from carving out a piece of the new empire for themselves.

DERBYNIWYD/ RECEIVED	~ 6 MAY 2005
CONWY	
GWYNEDD	
MÔN	
COD POST/POST CODE	LL55 1AS

The Man From Abilene

Leonard T. Knight

A Black Horse Western

ROBERT HALE · LONDON

© 1961, 2003 John Glasby
First hardcover edition 2003
Originally published in paperback as
The Man from Abilene by Chuck Adams

ISBN 0 7090 7248 1

Robert Hale Limited
Clerkenwell House
Clerkenwell Green
London EC1R 0HT

The right of John Glasby to be identified as
author of this work has been asserted by him
in accordance with the Copyright, Designs and
Patents Act 1988.

All characters in this book are fictional
and any resemblance to persons,
living or dead is purely coincidental

Typeset by
Derek Doyle & Associates, Liverpool.
Printed and bound in Great Britain by
Antony Rowe Limited, Wiltshire

ONE

HELL BENDER

Five miles out of Bluff Creek, the trail entered a narrow, steep-walled canyon and then came out into wild, open country. The dust from the trail came up in little red puffs under the horse's feet until Bart Nolan's throat and eyes were burning with it. Ahead, lay the emptiness of the desert where the only splashes of colour were the darting lizards which sped from rock to rock, deep purple creatures, some of which were bright green or crimson. Sometimes, he saw the slick grey of a rattler, but there was no other sound on the trail except the steady beat of the sorrel's hoofs on the hard ground.

He ran his keen-eyed gaze swiftly over the canyon wall as he rode through, probing the time-eroded sandstone face of it, lifting his head slightly to scan the covering of old cedars and brush. This was still wild, untamed country which abounded with outlaws and renegade army men who had fought in the Civil War and found the killing to their liking. Now they were out to get everything they could from this new territory which was just opening up. The frontier was wide open for settlement, but the killers and gamblers would inevitably come first.

He continued to search the broken boulders and rough country to the edge of the trail as he rode due west, sitting the saddle easily, wearing his guns low, his hands resting loosely on the pommel in front of him. He was a tall man for that country, slimly built, with a lean, handsome face and restless eyes that were hard and blue. He crossed two low ridges and a creek which was almost dry. The sun beat down upon him like the rays of hell, but he did not seem to notice it.

Towards evening, he reached the end of the bad country where the trail wound in and out of the canebreak. He jerked the head of the sorrel round and pulled him on to the trail. The horse's hoofs crunched loudly in the cane and down here, the trail wound in and out of the tall, rising stalks so that it would be easy for a man to get himself lost. Fortunately, the sorrel had travelled through country like this many times before and picked its way, sure-footed through the otherwise solid wall of cane. There was no sign that anyone had been this way for some time, but Nolan kept his eyes alert for the next half an hour. He followed the trail for half a mile or so, as it twisted and wound frequently, so narrow in places that it would have been impossible for two men to have ridden abreast.

Then, suddenly, he stopped the sorrel. There was the smell of wood smoke on the breeze. It was almost dark and he guessed that whoever was up ahead of him had lit a fire for the night. Nashville was still the best part of twenty miles away to the south-west and there was no other settlement worthy of note, although here and there, on the range beyond the canebreak, a few hardy settlers had thrown up wire over the trail and were attempting to tame the land.

Slipping from the saddle, he went forward cautiously on foot, the six-gun held in his right hand. He deliberately kept it there as he made his way through the brush for in the dead past there had been times when he had been jumped from the brush and he could see no sense in walking into trouble with his eyes shut.

When he reached the small clearing in the canebreak, he saw at once that there would be no trouble. A buck-shirted man, short and stocky, lay on his face beside the remains of the fire. Nolan went down on one knee beside him, felt for the heartbeat but could find none. Then he whipped up the man's shirt. Across the bare back were several red welts raised by a whip and just to the left of the backbone, standing out against the flesh, was a small black hole with a little blood still oozing out of the middle of it.

He stood up and looked across the canebreak. There was no sound of horses and in that country, he could see for less than a quarter of a mile. The shot which had killed this man could have come from anywhere. There was no sign of powder burns on the man's shirt and he figured that whoever had shot him had done so from a distance. But that didn't explain the whipmarks on the man's back. His lips tightened into white lines as he stared down at the man's body.

There was no sign of the dead man's horse but that went for nothing. Whoever had killed him could have brought him out here, whipped him and then shot him in the back, taking his horse back with them. He looked back up the trail and his eyes glittered momentarily. Bending, he lifted the man across his own saddle, swung up easily behind him and cut along the trail.

Two days later, Bart Nolan rode into Nashville. The town was growing fast since he had last seen it. Then, caught between the North and the South in the Civil War, it had been the scene of some of the bloodiest fighting in the entire struggle. Now, it seemed to be settling down again, but in spite of this, he could detect an undercurrent

7

of tension in the hot, dusty sunlight. The stage station stood across from the saloon, but he passed them both and rode straight to the sheriff's office beside the jail-house. The cowhands seated along the wooden frontwalk, watched him curiously, more intent on the dead man strung across his saddle than on himself.

In front of the sheriff's office, he dismounted, tethered the sorrel, and went inside, conscious of the eyes that followed his every move. The sheriff glanced up, squinting in the half-light inside the office. It was plain that he'd been drinking, the way his eyes looked kind of filmy, but he stood his ground with his legs braced wide apart and didn't sway a bit.

'Lookin' fer somebody, stranger?'

'You the sheriff of this town?' said Nolan thinly.

The other nodded. 'That's right.' His voice was wary and the film was suddenly gone from his eyes as he looked the other up and down appraisingly.

'There's a dead man outside over my saddle. I thought you might like to take a look at him. He's been shot in the back.'

The sheriff's eyes narrowed just a shade. 'You shoot him?' he asked abruptly.

'Nope. I found him along the trail to the east, in the canebreak about twenty miles from here. Looked as though he'd been whipped before he'd been shot.'

The sheriff nodded. 'I'll take a look at him.'

They went outside. A crowd had gathered around the sorrel. Nolan heard muttering but pretended not to notice it. The sheriff pulled back the buckskin shirt. The expression on his face did not alter as he stared down at the striped back and the small bullet-hole just below the shoulder blades. Then he pulled the man's head round to take a good look at his face.

'Joel Benson. Figgered it might be him,' said the sheriff

in a calm, almost disinterested voice. He let the man's head drop again. Then he looked up at Nolan. 'Where you from, stranger? How come you happened to find Benson like this?'

'Couldn't very well miss him,' replied the other evenly. 'He was lying in the middle of the trail beside the remains of a fire. I smelled wood smoke as soon as I entered the canebreak. Didn't take me long to find him. Figgered he hadn't come out from Bluff Creek. No trail leading that way. Guessed he must have come from this direction so I took a chance and brung him in. You say you know him?'

'That's right.' The sheriff nodded grimly. 'But you ain't answered the first part of my question yet. Where you from?'

'Way back east. First time I've been in these parts. Once got close to it during the war. Just ridin' through now on my way down to Texas.'

The sheriff, who had not taken his eyes off Nolan, said quietly out of the corner of his mouth, 'Okay, boys, reckon you can take him down off that saddle now. In the meantime, this saddle tramp has some explainin' to do. Reckon you'd better come inside, mister. Unless you want to give some trouble.'

His eyes were narrowed to mere slits. The first of the men came into view on Nolan's left, edging forward towards the sorrel. Another stepped down off the front-walk. Between them, then lifted the dead man from the pommel and carried him into the office.

Nolan shrugged. There were probably rifles trained on him at that very moment, he decided. Not that he wanted any gunplay at the moment. Things were just getting interesting and he figured that he'd string along with the sheriff for the time being until he had learned a little more about this man Benson, who had met his death in such a strange way on the trail.

Inside the office, the sheriff said too casually. 'Bein' a stranger around here, you won't know how things are in Nashville.'

'Somethin' I oughta know?'

'Could be. Jeb Saunders runs this place. Has a spread about two miles west of here. Two, mebbe three thousand head. Best prime beef.'

'So you figger he might have killed this cowhand, Benson'?'

'I didn't say that. If you value your health, you won't say it either. Jeb Saunders is a pretty big man as far as Nashville is concerned. I'm only telling you this fer your own good. I don't have to. But there was bad blood between Saunders and Benson. And he was no cowhand. Had a ranch a little way outa here, along the trail a piece. Upstream from Jeb's place.'

Nolan inclined his head, but said nothing, waiting for the other to continue.

The sheriff seemed to grin faintly. 'I can guess what you're thinking, and I reckon there might have been some rustling between the two, and I know for a fact that Benson tried to dam the stream so that there was no water for Saunders. But it went deeper than that. A lot deeper. You're in the Deep South now, stranger. Sure, the war's been over for the best part of five years, but not down here. Things are still much the same as in those days. The South is still at war with the North and Benson came from the North. Tried to settle here when the war was finished. He was an old army man, Captain, I reckon. There was talk once that he lit outa the army with over ten thousand dollars of Government money.'

'And then he set himself up here?' Nolan lifted an interrogatory brow.

'That's right. Jeb Saunders didn't like it. His family have been in these parts for nearly a century. Wasn't going to

10

have a damned Yankee holdin' the whip hand over him. But I never figgered it would come to murder.'

'There's no proof that he was to my way of thinking.'

'No. I guess not.' The other's voice was brittle as he went on: 'But you seem to be asking a lot of questions for a stranger in these parts. You wouldn't have an interest in either of these parties, would you, mister?'

'That's my business, Sheriff.' Nolan said.

'Mebbe, mebbe not. We don't like strangers coming into town and makin' trouble. Besides, I reckon I ought to warn you. There's a lot of people in town, pretty important people, who sided with Benson in his fight with Jeb Saunders. They might not take too kindly to his killer.'

'You suggesting that I might have killed him?' Bart snapped.

The sheriff spread his hands. 'Don't get me wrong, stranger. If I figgered it that way, I'd have you inside the jail right now. But it ain't what I think that counts around here. It's what the citizens of Nashville think. They get a little jumpy when there's a stranger around, particularly anybody who doesn't want to give his name. They figger he might have somethin' to hide.'

Bart Nolan frowned. For an instant, his hands rested on the long-barrelled sixes in the holsters slung low on his hips, then he relaxed. 'I guess I can take care of myself, Sheriff.' He moved towards the door, then turned. 'Just one thing. If I should decide to pay a visit to Jeb Saunders, where'd I find his spread?'

'Take the west trail leading outa town. About two, three miles you'll find his spread. Thinkin' of throwing in your hand with Jeb Saunders?'

'Could be. I'll think it over.' He strode out of the sheriff's office and mounted up. Slowly, he rode along the main street of the town, conscious of the stares of the men on the sidewalks. It seemed odd that a stranger should

11

attract so much attention, but he guessed that word had got around already that he had brought in the body of Joel Benson. He wondered vaguely what Jeb Saunders was thinking right at that moment. No doubt word had got through to him of what had happened. In Nashville, news seemed to travel fast.

At midday, he came to the Saunders's spread outside of town. It lay in a long valley, flanked by tall, rising hills, topped with clusters of pine with wire stretched across the trail, barring his path. At the south end, the valley broadened out and the hills paced away into the distance and still he was forced to ride along the wire. At the very end of the valley, he reined the sorrel and squinted his eyes against the sun. A movement, off to one side, caught his eye immediately. The two men were riding a higher trail, inside the boundary fence, against the mesa and were heading towards him. He waited, then rode out boldly into the open.

They approached warily, one man tall and big. Nolan guessed that he'd go well over two hundred pounds with mighty little fat to it. He wore a broad, flat-topped hat and looked like a man who always seemed to know exactly what he wanted to do, and who did it in spite of all opposition. The other man who rode a little way behind the first, was of a different breed altogether. Nolan recognized his type immediately. A gunslinger of the worst type, ready to hire out his gun to anyone who paid the right price. No doubt, in some state or other, there would be a price on his head, but at the moment, Bart Nolan wasn't concerned with collecting any bounty money that might be offered for this killer, dead or alive.

'You know whose land this is?' demanded the big man harshly. He reined his horse roughly on the opposite side of the fence and stared at Nolan from beneath lowered brows.

'From what I was told back in Nashville, I guess it belongs to Jeb Saunders,' said Nolan mildly.

'Then you heard aright,' nodded the other. 'I'm Jeb Saunders. I own the whole of this valley as far as you can see.'

Bart saw the speculation in the other's eyes. The situation was obviously puzzling him. Finally, he said thinly: 'You lookin' for a job, stranger?'

'I might be, if there was one going,' he agreed. 'Maybe I'd better first tell you somethin' about myself. You'll probably hear all about it pretty soon from town.'

'No hurry.' The big man nodded, taking a quick look at the guns hanging in their holsters. 'Handy with a gun?'

'Fair.' Bart studied the other through narrowed eyes. Deep down inside, he wondered what was coming next. Knowing a little of this man's reputation, he figured that there would always be an opportunity on the ranch for another hired gunman. A man such as Jeb Saunders was bound to have a heap of enemies, especially in Nashville, even though it was reckoned that he had the town in his pocket. He half-suspected that the sheriff was in his pay too, but at the moment, he had little proof of that. He would have to go warily for the time being.

'You look like a man who can handle himself if there was to be trouble. I need men like that. It isn't easy out here, and since the war things have started to go from bad to worse. The settlers are moving in along the trails, carving out huge pieces of the open range. We'd like to talk peacefully with them, but they won't listen to us. Stubborn as mules. So we have to fight them in the only way we know how. With guns.'

Nolan shrugged his broad shoulders. 'I can use these guns if I have to,' he said slowly, chewing on the words. 'Right now, I'm just moseying through. If the pay is right, I might consider staying here awhile.'

'A hundred dollars a month with chow.'

'That seems fair enough,' said Nolan quietly. Again there came that sense of wariness and he looked at the other man sharply.

'Aren't you taking a big chance on him, boss?'asked the gunman thinly. His lips were curled back, showing his teeth. 'We don't know anything about him. He may be nothin' more than a saddletramp working his way through. But then, he might just be a—'

'That's enough, Sutton, I do the hiring and firing of men around here and what I say still goes. I like the look of him and he's hired.' He turned back and threw a piercing glance at Nolan. 'I reckon the next few days will tell me everything I want to know.'

Once through the wire, Nolan followed the others across the open range. He rode a little way behind the two men, studying them from under lowered lids. There was no denying that Jeb Saunders had more energy and purpose in him than any other half dozen men Brad had ever known. It was more than possible that he had given the order to kill Joel Benson, even if it had not been his finger that had pulled the trigger. Saunders would never allow any man to stand in his way. For him, there never had been and never would be but one way to go – his.

There was plenty of beef on the range and plenty of men too. Another half hour and they were riding over a low ridge, wooded with sassafras and hickory. In front of them, in the long meadows, the blue grass grew thick and succulent. Bart looked about him keenly. On the higher ground, beyond the large ranch-house and outbuildings, where the spring-fed stream which came rushing down from further along the edge of the valley – in the direction where he guessed the Benson place to lie – was rich corn land. But there was very little corn being grown there. Obviously Saunders was a cattle man, plain and simple.

He grew aware that Saunders had reined his mount and was staring back at him intently.

He said thinly: 'I reckon you must have ridden through the town before you came out here. Could be that you heard some talk in there about this feud of mine with Joel Benson.'

'Some,' admitted Bart cautiously. 'Seems he was damming the stream higher up, stopping the water.'

'More than that. He was rustling my cattle, changing the brand from the Lazy V to the Circle W. I've seen range wars before and there's nothin' worse. I figured I might have to do something to stop this one before it really got started. Seems now, though, that I've been saved the trouble. One of my hands rode in from town a whiles back with the news that Benson had been brought in by some saddletramp who claimed to have picked up his body fifteen miles to the east of Nashville.' There was a little quirk to his brows as he went on sharply. 'You wouldn't be that saddletramp, would you?'

'Reckon I might.'

'That's what I thought. Mind telling me how it happened? As you can guess, I'm interested. I'd be a fool if I didn't guess what they're saying about me in town. They'll be figuring that I killed him because of this bad feeling between the two of us.'

'Somebody killed him. Matters little to me who it was. I just found him and brought him in.'

For a moment, he thought he noticed a look of relief flash over the other's hard features, but it was gone so quickly that he couldn't be absolutely sure. Saunders nodded as if satisfied.

'Sutton will show you where you'll bunk, and tell you what your work will be. I may want to see you again. I like to know a little more about the men I hire than I do about you.'

15

In the early hours of the morning, the drumming of running horses brought Bart Nolan awake. He rolled over in his blankets inside the bunkhouse, then sat up swiftly, silently. The rest of the men were still asleep. He strained his eyes into the darkness, trying to make out Sutton's shape inside his blankets, but the space where he usually bedded down was empty. He sat up then, no longer sleepy. The sound of the horses stopped, then continued again. But it was a wraith, oddly elusive, and it was difficult for him to tell from which direction it came.

Smoothly, quietly, he slid out of his blankets, stood up and went over to the window of the bunkhouse, looking out into the darkness. There was yellow moonlight spilling over the ground, making a multitude of shadows around the ranch itself. As he stood there, he thought he heard the sound of guns, but he couldn't be sure. The riders, whoever they were, had been heading towards the ranch, but had then turned northwards again, heading out towards the open range. The hoofs that had drummed through the yellow moonlight, were thudding into the distance now and he debated whether to bed down again, when he saw the tall, dark figure coming from the direction of the ranch. Something born of more than curiosity kept him standing there for a long moment, until he recognized the figure which strode purposefully towards the bunkhouse. It was Sutton, the gunslinger.

He paused only for a fraction of a second, then swiftly went back to his blankets and rolled himself up in them, feigning sleep. Sutton came into the bunkhouse on cat feet, paused for a brief moment in the doorway looking carefully about him. Then he glanced back towards the ranch, raised his right hand slowly in signal to someone there, closed the door silently. Going to his own blankets, he stretched himself out, rolled over once or twice, then lay still.

Bart turned things over in his mind. Events were beginning to add up to what he had expected. It was no accident that he had ridden out here and asked for a job with the Lazy V. Louisiana was a big state and a wild one, full of coyotes who were determined to carve out an empire of their own, right here, to rake in all of the wealth there was, run their illicit gambling saloons in the towns, promote their own men into the positions of the law – in general, to run everything in their own way. Jeb Saunders was a man such as this. A man with big ideas and with the means to back those ideas to the hilt.

Sooner or later, the homesteaders would begin to move in, reaching out westwards, through Texas and on to the rich lands of California. Many of them would come this way, along the trails which led through Louisiana and some would squat here and try to build new lives for themselves in this rich country. But men such as Jeb Saunders would never allow that to happen without a fight, because the squatters would bring with them law and order, would fence off the range, plough the land, and whittle away the power of the big cattle barons. He wondered what Saunders' reactions would be if he once suspected that the man he had just hired, the man he thought was nothing more than a saddletramp, was in reality a deputy U.S. marshal. Sooner or later, it would have to come out, but until then, he would have to bide his time, keep his identity a secret if possible, until he had all of the evidence he needed to convict this man Saunders. It wasn't going to be easy. He had no illusions on that particular score. The sheriff back in Nashville hadn't exaggerated when he had claimed that Saunders was the uncrowned king of this country. His influence clearly extended far beyond the boundary wire of the Lazy V spread. He suspected that, if he went back into Nashville, he would find that all of the saloons, the gambling dens, and possibly the sheriff himself, were run by the same man. It made things doubly difficult. There might come a time when he would have to take someone into his confidence, but with most of the lawmen in the pay of Jeb Saunders and possibly everyone else going in fear of him, it would be next to impossible to find a man he could trust.

He frowned thoughtfully in the darkness. Joel Benson might have been such a man. Clearly he had come out into the open against Saunders, but now he had paid for that with his life. His face grew grim with remembering. What had become of the Benson spread now? he wondered. Was there still someone up there determined to carry on the fight? He rolled over more comfortably into his blankets, listened for a moment to the quiet breathing of the other men in the bunkhouse, then closed his eyes. Perhaps he might learn something more in the morning. This was a violent country, still divided between north and south, with the old hatreds just beneath the surface, ready to flare up again, especially after the untimely death of Joel Benson. Violence was like a stone pitched into water. It formed a ripple and then more growing circles, spreading out in all directions. There was bound to be more violence. Benson's death had been just the beginning. There would be more to come and who could tell how far the ripples would reach or who they would touch?

The next morning, Nolan stepped inside the cookshack and threw a swift glance down the long, wooden table. Sutton, the gunslinger was missing. He narrowed his eyes as he looked along the other men around the table. There was nothing on their faces or in their glances to show that they had any idea of what had happened during the night. He took his place along the table and ate heartily. The chow was good and the coffee hot and strong. A little while later, the door opened and Sutton came in. He threw a swift, enigmatic glance at Nolan, then took his place at the top of the table. There had been something in that glance which sent a little quiver through Bart's stomach muscles.

18

He smiled slightly. Obviously the other was puzzled. Clearly he wanted to know a lot more about Bart. Towards the end of the meal he glanced up sharply with suspicious eyes and said thinly: 'Just where's you from, stranger? You ride in here and ask for a job after bringing in Benson's body from somewhere out east. How do we know you didn't kill him?'

Bart thinned his lips. 'You don't,' he said shortly. 'As for the rest, I come from Abilene. The name's Nolan. Bart Nolan.'

'Nolan,' mused the other. There was a speculative look in his eyes. He was running through all of the names in his mind, trying to place him, figured Bart, His face darkened. 'You're a long way from your own stamping territory, aren't you?'

'Once the war finished, I couldn't settle,' said Bart easily. 'Just drifted, taking a job here, another there. Cow-punching. Once I was a dealer in a saloon. They even tried to make me a deputy sheriff in Dodge.' Sutton nodded. Whether the answers satisfied him or not, it was impossible to tell from his expression. But he asked no further questions and sat sullenly at the table, chewing his food reflectively.

The week that followed was one of hard work and equally hard riding. The Lazy V spread was as large as the sheriff had said and Bart guessed there were close on five thousand head of prime cattle there. For the time being, Sutton seemed to have lost his interest in Bart and the U.S. marshal found himself doing all of the hard work of a cowboy. But in doing so, he kept his eyes and ears open and learned a great deal about Jeb Saunders, of the men he had hired and the men who hated him. There was the usual talk in the bunkhouse at night, whenever Sutton was absent, on the range during the day, and piece by piece, the picture began to fit together. There were still bits missing from the overall pattern, but sufficient was there for him to see the general position on the Lazy V.

Saunders had been a colonel in the Civil War and had fought bitterly against the North then, and ever since. His family had owned this land for the past hundred years or so, but there was talk that, shortly before the war, the family fortunes had been at a particularly low ebb. A series of droughts had reduced the number of cattle on the spread to less than three hundred head. Then had come the war. Saunders had distinguished himself during the early days of the fighting, but little was known of his career as the war had drawn to its inevitable close. That part of his life seemed to be shrouded in mystery.

But there had been a sudden and inexplicable change in the family fortunes. It wasn't long before Jeb Saunders had bought out, or chased out, the other ranch holders in the valley, and had owned all of it himself. All of it, that was, apart from the Benson spread. Joel Benson had arrived in Nashville shortly after the end of the war. A Northerner, he had earned the instant dislike of Jeb Saunders. A dislike which had turned into a fierce hatred when the Northerner had refused to sell his spread with its effective control of the water supply to the valley. The feud had flared up intermittently during the ensuing years, with charges of rustling being laid by each man against the other and constant gun battles between the hired gunslammers on both sides. Now that Benson was dead, it seemed only a question of time before Saunders was, indeed, undisputed king of the whole valley and of the town itself.

The Lazy V crew itself was all that Bart had expected it to be. They worked the range, herded the beef, checked the wire around the spread. But word had also gone out over the grapevine that gunslammers were needed here and they were drifting in from all over the State. Saunders seemed to be hiring them all, without question, keeping them for some future use known only to himself. The greater number of them spent their time in Nashville, in the saloons, or loafed away their time in the bunkhouse, doing very little of the work on the ranch.

Towards the end of the week, Bart saw Saunders ride out with Sutton and a dozen of the toughest gunslammers. The band was gone for almost two days. When they arrived back, saddle-worn and dust-stained, Saunders was grimly pleased. That night, the word was spread in the bunkhouse.

'There's been trouble at the northern end of the valley. A couple of the range families had come out into the open and declared themselves against Saunders, naming him as Joel Benson's killer. They had attempted to bring some of the other ranchers in with them and Saunders had struck viciously, before they could become a menace to him.'

Bart tried to find out something more. Hank Willard, a tall, flame-haired cowboy, stood leaning against a post outside the bunkhouse, rolling a quirly. He edged over to him. 'What's all this leading up to, Hank? Any idea?' The other shrugged, then his face darkened.

'Plenty trouble is brewin' in these parts now, Bart. Yuh heard about Sutton and the others moving out two days ago.'

'Sure. Saw 'em leave myself. What happened?'

'They rode over to the Thompson outfit, shot old man Thompson, his wife and two sons, then fired the ranch. Reckon it would burn like tinder. They brung back most of the Thompson herd with 'em. They're down at the creek now.'

'You figger we'll see any action around here ourselves?' He didn't know how far he could trust this man and perhaps every single word of this conversation would soon get back to Saunders, so he had to be careful what he said.

'Could be.' Willard flicked a match, drew deeply on the quirly. 'Jeb isn't pullin' in all of these gunslammers fer nothin'. He's aiming to git the whole of this valley fer himself. There was talk a whiles back of a U.S. marshal on his way here, but we've seen nothin' of him in these parts, so I reckon it was just talk. But Jeb's takin' no chances. Pretty soon, he'll have the biggest army of gunslammers in the State.'

'I've been watching the men he's been bringing in over the past few days. Some of 'em I recognise.'

'Most of 'em are wanted dead or alive in some state or other,' admitted Willard. 'Jess Ordway rode in yesterday. He's reckoned to be one of the fastest guns in the west. The Mexican Kid's here too. Rode in a couple days ago. Can't say I like working with men like that. This is going to be a bad and bloody range war when it starts, and there's nobody here can stop it. Mebbe if they were to send in a detachment of State troopers it might solve things, but the army's been disbanded for five years.'

'What about the Benson spread?'

Willard threw him a swift glance, then grinned tightly. 'Don't reckon they can do anythin' now. With Joel Benson out of the way, the rest of the family can't fight Saunders.'

Bart's dark brows arched. 'There is a family then?'

'Shore. His daughter runs the place now, or tries to. She won't get many hands with her father dead. Jeb has the whip hand now and everybody knows it. It ain't going to be healthy working for Reva Benson now. She'll have to sell pretty soon and the price ain't going to be very high.'

Bart nodded. He felt the grim premonition of savage violence about to break in the very near future, and he would be right in the middle of it. There would be more complications and it looked bad enough already. He didn't want to overplay his hand, but that might happen if he were forced to show it too soon. Jeb Saunders had seen this trouble brewing for quite a while now and had gathered together the biggest and most formidable army of gunslammers and vicious killers the west had ever known.

There was a sudden movement in the yard outside the

bunkhouse. Sutton came striding across. His grey-flecked eyes still held that suspicious look as he said:

'Nolan. The boss wants a word with you. You'll find him over by the ranch house. Better get there *pronto*.'

Bart nodded. He found Jeb Saunders in front of the ranch-house, talking with a couple of his hired killers. Even as he approached, Saunders said something in a low voice to the two men and they ambled off in the direction of the cookshack, one of them – the Mexican Kid – throwing Bart a guarded look over his shoulder as he moved lithely away. Even though he was a Mexican, Bart noticed that the other wore gringo range garb. His guns were tied down and there was the image of death in his eyes and once again, Bart wondered why he was there. Evidently the killer breed was back in command now that the war was finished and there hadn't been time to establish a proper system of law and order in this frontier of the west.

'You probably heard about the trouble we had with the Thompsons, Nolan,' said Saunders quickly. His eyes were deep and appraising. 'We've had trouble like this before and I reckon we'll have a lot more of it before this town and the range around it is settled and set on its feet.'

'You got anything in mind for stopping it before it gets outa hand?' asked Bart tightly. He forced his voice into evenness.

'Could be. But that ain't none of your concern at the moment. I need most of my men here for the next day or so. That means you'll have to watch the cattle I've got down at the creek. I want you there first thing tomorrow morning. I've got a couple of my boys down there right now, but there may be trouble, so keep your eyes open and your guns handy. You understand?'

Bart nodded. He understood all right. There was going to be more trouble, but Saunders still did not trust him. So he was to be kept out of the way until it had blown over.

And the best way of doing that, without arousing too much suspicion in his own mind, was to pack him off to the far edge of the range, to watch over a bunch of cows, with probably the other two men to keep an eye, not only on the cows, but on himself.

'This job may take a little gunplay, but that's what I hired you for,' said Saunders heavily.

Bart looked up quickly at the other. 'If you want me to smoke a man down in cold blood or do a drygulch on him, then count me out.'

'It's nothin' like that,' interjected the other hastily. He turned to leave. All trace of expression had been wiped from his heavy features. His bulging eyes had a cunning glint in them as he paused, then went on slowly: 'The war did a lot for me, Nolan. It set me back where I was before. I know it's funny for a Southerner to make a statement like that, but that's the way it happened. I made several thousand dollars selling beef to the Confederate Army and now there are men who're trying to step in and take away everything I built up in those years. That isn't going to happen, Nolan. You understand that.'

'Sure, I understand, Mr. Saunders.'

The other chuckled drily. 'I reckon we're going to get on well together, Nolan. Help me and you'll find that I have influence in these parts which can do a man a lot of good. All of this talk of the army moving into Nashville is just smoke in the wind. It don't mean a thing.'

'What about the sheriff? Ain't he going to do anything about it?'

'He'll do exactly as I tell him.' Saunders beamed broadly as if the whole situation should be perfectly clear to Nolan. 'I'm buying out the Benson spread now that Joel's dead. Once I have my hands on that, I'll be in a position to face anybody here, even the Army if they ever decide to come.'

TWO

DUEL ON THE RANGE

Early the following morning, before sun-up, Brad lit out for the far edge of the range. He had that rendezvous with the two cowpokes at the creek and there was the bitter knowledge in him that while he was away, Saunders was planning something else, some other act which he felt he ought to know about. The trail took him northwards across wide rangelands that lay like green carpeting in the early light of dawn. When the sun rose, the day was good and warm but with no sense of oppression in its heat and the sky was both wide and cloudless over his head, touching the purple hills in the distance. He had chosen the high route deliberately. Saunders would expect him to stick to the low trail. But Bart had figured that if anyone was trailing him, the sooner he knew about it, the better. From here, he could look down over the valley and see the trail, where it wound back across the range towards the ranch behind him.

For a long time the trail had been empty, but a little before noon, he spotted the two riders moving up fast.

They rode with a purpose, but seemed to be cautious, as if shy of showing themselves to anyone on the trail ahead of them. They would also be puzzled men, reflected Brad with a grim amusement. They would have expected to have sighted him long before this. Soon, they might even figure out that he had taken the high trail and then they would come looking for him there, checking on his movements. Jeb Saunders hadn't got where he had by taking unnecessary chances. He would want to know for certain that this man from Abilene had reached the creek and was well out of the way in case of trouble.

A mile further on, the trail dipped off the ridge and swung left through a narrow, little valley that evidently opened out into the main spread a few miles ahead. Bart drew rein at the head of the narrow gap which wound downwards through the hills. Slowly, his eyes swept over the range below him. The two horsemen were riding slowly now, looking for his trail.

He figured they would ride a little way yet before they decided that he had taken the other trail. Then it would take an hour or so for them to come up across country. He unsaddled at the point where the creek ran down the hillside, splashing through the pines. He found the silence of the pines a balm, giving him a chance to think things out, to plan ahead. With Joel Benson dead – and with no attempt on the sheriff's part to try to find the killer it was more than likely that Saunders would gain control of the spread to the west and with it, the whole of the valley. Then he would undoubtedly move into Nashville in force, take over everything quite openly and declare himself head of this empire.

More than once, he thought about Benson's daughter. This was no place for a woman, not with all hell about to be let loose on the range and he figured that she would be forced to sell at any price Saunders offered. There was

26

nobody else in the state who would dare to buy the spread in the face of Jeb Saunders' offer. He ate some of the food in his saddlebag, washed it down with water from the creek. Then he watered the sorrel, tightened the girth of the saddle and swung himself up into it. In that same moment, the bark of a rifle broke the silence and there was the vicious hum of the bullet, like an angry hornet, cutting through the air close to his head.

His reflex action saved his life. Throwing himself sideways, he slid out of the saddle, hit the ground with a blow that knocked most of the wind from his lungs, then rolled several times until he hit the water in the creek. There was the savage sound of a second shot but by the time the echoes had died away among the pines, he was worming his way out of the water, along the bank of the creek, his gun out of leather, eyes and eyes straining to pick out the position of the drygulcher.

He attained the cover of a clump of trees, slithered like a snake into them, seeking a pattern in the shadows. Behind him, he heard the sorrel snicker and knew that the sidewinder who had ambushed him was still there and that he had a mount hidden some place nearby. He wrapped caution around him then, sliding from one patch of shadow to the next and soon he had the sensation that the man he sought was very close by although he could see no one. Here, in the pines were hunter and hunted, but at the moment it was difficult to say which was which. He crossed a small coulee where some tiny spring had run itself dry in the past, crossed over it noiselessly. He made his guess where the sidewinder might be, headed around that point in a wide arc, making no sound as he padded catlike through the trees. He could sense the crawl of excitement within him as he edged forward. So far, he couldn't see the other, but he had an excellent idea of where he was, crouched within the shadow of the trees

27

some thirty yards to the right. His guess had been right; he had calculated the odds against him, but the rest had to be left to chance.

He moved into another clump of trees, coming out behind the spot where he figured the man was hiding. Then he caught sight of the other's mount, a bay gelding, tethered to a low bush. It was a mount he didn't recognize, certainly he had never seen it at the Lazy V ranch, but that didn't mean a thing. If Jeb Saunders had chosen this method of getting rid of him, he was due for an unpleasant surprise. Cautiously, he edged forward until he came within sight of the man who lay in the tall scrub with his back to him. The other was obviously puzzled by what had happened. Bart smiled grimly to himself. The drygulcher was clearly deliberating whether or not to move forward, to check on whether he had killed his victim. Very carefully, Bart sheathed his gun. He wanted this man alive if possible and now that he had the advantage, he had to keep it. If Saunders was planning something like this, the sooner he knew about it, the better.

If the man heard him coming, he had scant warning. He must have sensed Bart moving in on him for he whirled in the instant before Bart leapt. His gun came up, the barrel rising swiftly, instinctively, but before he could take proper aim, Bart's foot lashed out, kicking the gun from the other's grasp. It exploded harmlessly as the man's finger tightened on it convulsively, the bullet humming over Bart's head and losing itself in the distance. The broad, coarse face flamed with anger and sudden realization and the man's action was instinctively quick as he rolled sideways, bringing his right foot up in the same movement. It caught Bart on the side of the leg, threw him slightly off balance. Staggering, he came upright once more, swung round as the other gained his feet and came rushing in, lips thinned viciously, teeth just showing in the shadow of his face. His head snapped back savagely as Bart's fist smashed into it and for a moment, the other seemed to get tangled up in his own feet as he swayed backward. He hit the ground hard and for a moment, looked up, his face twisted hard in amazement and anger, his bloody features twisted in surprise.

Bart waited, staring down at him. For a moment, the other seemed to be deliberating whether or not to try to make a dive for his gun, lying in the scrub a couple of yards away. Bart watched him carefully, his right hand hovering over his own iron. Then the other scrambled to his feet, stood swaying drunkenly for a moment before hurling himself forward with a sudden, surprising speed.

Bart lashed two hammering blows at the other's face as he came in and blood spurted once more from just below his right eye. But as he swung in a third blow, the other sensed it and jerked his head back and to one side so that Bart's fist merely scraped across the length of the man's jaw. The other grunted, then lowered his head and came in like a battering ram. The blow took Bart full in the chest, knocking him backward on to the ground. Twisting as he fell, Bart clutched at the other's right wrist, and pulled sharply with all of his strength. The man flew over his shoulders and hit the ground hard.

Swiftly, Nolan rolled over and pushed himself to his feet. The other was already getting to his and there was a dangerous glint in the muddy eyes. His thick lips were drawn back from the yellowed teeth but for all his surprise and anger, he did not rush in blindly now. Rather, he moved forward in a wrestler's crouch, arms outspread slightly, fingers curled into talons. He started circling slowly, eyes never leaving Bart's face. Then, abruptly, he charged. Without pause, Bart smashed two further blows to the other's split mouth, but the man seemed to absorb the punishment and his big arms swung outwards and circled Bart's body, tightening their grip instinctively. They closed with the force of a bear hug before the other could wriggle himself clear.

Now, he knew, it was to be a fight to the finish. He knew what was coming with those arms locked tightly behind his back. The other would put on the pressure and snap his back like a rotten twig. Fighting to suck air down into his heaving lungs, he hammered away at the other's face with his fists, but the drygulcher merely lowered his head until it was pressed hard into Bart's chest and kept it there, increasing the pressure which would eventually break Bart Nolan's back.

There were to be no ethics to this fight, thought Bart savagely. The other meant to kill him. Swiftly, he changed his mode of attack. Stamping downwards with his heel, he struck the other hard on the top of the right foot. The man uttered a sharp grunt of pain and the pressure in the encircling arms slackened a little. Bart drew in a gasp of air, then struck viciously at the man's head, at the same time relaxing the muscles of his legs. The other fell forward slightly as Bart's weight pulled at his body, throwing him off balance. As he struggled desperately to keep on his feet, Bart snapped another hammer blow on the back of the man's neck, twisting his body savagely at the same time. The arms around his body were loosened a little more and he could breathe more easily. Keeping the advantage, he brought up his right knee, hit the other in the pit of the stomach and, as he fell back, gasping with pain, clipped a hard drive to the other's jaw. The man's clawing fingers tried for a hold on his body, ripped at his shirt for a moment, then fell away and he collapsed on to the scrub, gasping savagely for breath, hands clutching at his face.

A quick glance told him that the other was beaten for the time being, but Bart was taking no further chances. He picked up the gun which lay a few feet away and pushed it into his belt. Then he went over to the man on the ground, saw that the eyes were open but filmed with pain.

'Now, buster,' he gritted savagely, 'I reckon you've got a mite of explainin' to do. Why did you try to drygulch me back there? If this is the way Jeb Saunders tries to get rid of men he doesn't want, he'd better send somebody out the next time who can do the job properly. I've got a good mind to kill you right now.'

The man started to answer and then a voice sounded behind them, close in. 'Just keep where you are, mister and don't make any false moves, else this gun's sure liable to go off.'

He had no option but to obey and Bart cursed himself inwardly for not having had the sense to figure out that there had been probably two of them, but it wasn't this which surprised him so much as the fact that it had been a woman's voice that had spoken.

'All right,' said the voice again. 'Now get up and turn round slowly and carefully but keep your hands where I can see them.'

Keeping his hands in full view, he turned round to face the girl as she stepped forward out of the cover of a brush thicket, a cocked rifle in her hands. The barrel was pointed straight at his chest and one look at her face told him that she would use it if necessary.

Bart said: 'You'll be Joel Benson's daughter.'

She nodded shortly. 'That's right. And we already know who you are. Bart Nolan, the snake who shot my father in the back. If I figured you'd get a proper trial, I'd take you back into Nashville and have you charged with murder. But I hear you've thrown in your lot with Saunders and that means the jury will be rigged so that you'll get off scott free. That being the case, I reckon we'd better shoot you now.'

'Now wait a minute,' Bart stared at her. 'You're crazy if

you think I shot your father. Sure, I found him on the trail from Bluff Creek, but he was dead when I stumbled across him. He'd been shot in the back and—'

'Shot in the back by you,' declared Reva Benson viciously. Bart saw her finger tighten on the trigger of the rifle. Behind him, he heard the other man getting to his feet, still gasping from the beating he had taken. He came round into view now, took away Bart's guns from their holsters, and pulled his own out of his belt.

Bart thought fast. Against a man he might have taken a chance, but with a determined and angry young woman such as this, he felt off balance. He grew aware that the other man was watching him closely as he wiped the blood off his face.

'Listen,' said Bart urgently. 'You've got to believe me when I say that I didn't kill your father. I never even knew him. After I picked him up on the trail, I brought him into Nashville because it was the nearest place to the spot where I found him, apart from Bluff Creek and there was no trail leading in that direction. I reported in to the sheriff. D'you reckon he would have let me go if he figured that I'd killed him?'

'He would if he was in Saunders' pay,' gritted the man thickly. He looked round at the girl. 'We'd better do what we have to do and git outa here, Reva,' he said hoarsely. 'This killer ain't alone. I spotted a couple his pals making their way along the low trail to the south. They'll have heard the shootin' by now and they'll be coming up this way to investigate. We don't want to be cornered on Saunders' territory. They'd shoot us down for sure.'

'I know it, Jed,' she hesitated. 'But I don't want to shoot a man in cold blood if there's any doubt.'

'Listen,' said the other thickly. 'You heard for yourself what they've been saying in town. It's all over Nashville that this here saddletramp killed your father. That's why he suddenly got this job workin' for Saunders. He don't take on nobody unless he's a professional killer. I've met this breed before.'

'Maybe I can convince you that I'm not the man who killed your father,' said Bart quietly. He wasn't sure how far he could trust these two, how far he could place his life in their hands, for that would be what he would be doing if he showed them the badge and the commission which was tucked away inside his riding boot. But if he was to have someone on his side, someone who hated Jeb Saunders and all he stood for, just as much as he did himself, then surely Reva Benson was that person.

'What kinda trick is this?' sneered the other harshly. He whirled on the girl. 'Don't listen to him, Miss Benson. He's just stallin' fer time until his two men get here.' His face showed a bitter hatred as he stared at Bart. He said: 'What kind of a goddam' fool do you take me for?'

'Listen, both of you,' Bart said and felt the sweat begin to trickle down his face as the other's finger took up some of the slack on the trigger of his six-gun. 'There isn't much time with those two men heading this way. D'you think that Jeb Saunders has been able to do all of this, build up his empire of murder and corruption without it coming to the attention of the State Governor? You won't be shooting a common killer if you shoot me, you'll be killing a U.S. Deputy Marshal and that's something you won't get away with no matter how far you try to run—'

'By God, Nolan,' snarled the other viciously. 'D'you think we believe such tales? If Miss Benson doesn't have the guts to kill you in cold blood, I do and I'm going to shoot you down here and now. But it ain't gonna be quick. You'll die slow like Miss Benson's father did when you whipped him before shooting him.'

'No! Hold it, Jed.' The girl's eyes glinted as she issued the order. She turned to face Bart. 'All right. Convince me that you're a U.S. Deputy Marshal – and hurry. If this is a trick to stall for time, you'll die just the same and it won't be an easy death.'

Bart dug into his riding boot, came up with the badge and commission. Under the watchful and disbelieving eye of the ranch foreman, he handed them over to the girl. She glanced at them closely and then gave them to the man.

'You could have killed the real marshal and taken these from his body,' said Jed hoarsely, reluctantly.

'I could. But I didn't.' Bart took them back and pushed them into the top of his riding boot again.

The girl made a slight gesture of her hand. 'Give him back his guns, Jed,' she said sharply and lowered the rifle. 'I reckon for once we made a mistake.' She looked keenly at Bart. 'You figure on working for Saunders until you've got all the evidence you need? I could use a man like you. If I don't get any help, I'll be forced to sell out to Saunders.'

'I've got a job to do, Miss Benson,' he said quietly. 'Part of it is to find out who did kill your father. But first, I've got to learn something more about Jeb Saunders. There's a lot I still don't know about him. Where he got all of the money to pay for this spread in the first place and stock it with so many cattle. Seems he must have got some money from somewhere just after the war finished.'

'If you need help, we'll do what we can,' said Reva Benson. 'But you'll find that you'll be on your own in Nashville. You'll get no help from the sheriff and the telegraph office will report all messages to Saunders. And don't forget that Saunders has something over you now. If you ever give him cause to want to get rid of you, he'll press for a murder charge on the grounds of killing my father. And the jury will be hand-picked, so what are you going to do about it?'

'Do?' he asked and some of his old resentment burned

brightly inside him again. 'There's nothing I can do at the moment. Until I have enough evidence to bring Saunders in front of a Grand Jury, my hands are tied. I've got to fall in with him and short of committing murder, I'll have to continue taking orders from him, anything to prevent him from becoming suspicious.'

She said dismally, 'Then there isn't much we can do to help you.' Her voice dropped lower. In the distance, he could hear the two riders calling to each other and there was the faint sound of their mounts pushing their way through the scrub as they came nearer.

'You'd better light outa here,' he said sharply in a hushed whisper, 'before those coyotes find you. They'll kill you for sure, if they find you on this range.'

He heard the quick intake of the girl's breath. She nodded. 'Are your horses fresh?' he asked tensely.

'They'll do,' the man said. His tone had lost some of its anger and resentment. 'They're closing in, I think.'

'I'll try to stall 'em off as long as I can,' muttered Bart. 'Better walk your horses through the trees alongside the trail and then cut north. You ought to make it to your own spread before they can catch up with you.'

They moved out a few moments later, walking their mounts into the trees. Bart stood quite still, then whistled up his own horse and swung himself easily into the saddle. His back and ribs still hurt where the other had crushed them with that bear-hug, but he held his saddler's reins loosely in his hands and leaned forward over the saddle. He could hear the faint, furtive movements of the other horses as they moved away into the trees to the north of the trail. The minutes ran on, piling up the silence until it seemed to have closed in around him like a blanket in which nothing moved and the only sound was that of his own heart thumping against his chest.

When he figured that Reva Benson and her foreman

had got well away, he touched spurs to his own mount and rode onward along the trail which threaded its way through the timber. As yet, he saw no sign of the two herders who had been following him. Had they cut north, hoping to outwit him, thinking that he himself had left the trail, and spotted them earlier and was trying to slip through unnoticed? He had now a new choice to make. To try to find those men, to get from them their reason for following him. He reasoned that he could do this, by force if necessary. Or he could ride straight on along the trail as if nothing had happened, and come out to the creek at sundown. If he did that, it would allay any suspicion that Saunders might have. He was very careful about his decision, first making sure that any pursuit of Reva Benson and Jed had been thrown off by them, before making up his mind. Then he pulled the head of the sorrel around sharply and cut off the trail, heading down the side of the hills. His body was weary and his brain was weary so that for a long while, he merely allowed the sorrel to have its head, not thinking.

He crossed the stage road which still ran through the Saunders' spread, although how much of a cut Jeb took for that privilege, he didn't know. All of his thinking was bleak when he finally came out of the timber as the sun was westering, throwing long shadows among the trees. He came upon a narrow, swiftly-flowing creek and stopped to give his horse a drink, taking one for himself. It would be sundown in another couple of hours and by that time, he had to be with the herd at the northern edge of the spread. Those two riders who had been so keen on following his trail that morning could have circled around him and by now, could be ahead of him. If he didn't show up on time, Saunders would hear of it and start asking questions.

He hit the trail which led northwards to the very edge

of the range in the last of the evening light, coming upon it out of one of the long stretches of open rangeland which were so numerous here. The herd lay in front of him, scattered in a loose bunch over the grassland. As he approached the men who had set up camp by the side of the creek, every dragging second seemed like an eternity. Bart dismounted, hobbled the sorrel, then strode towards the men, squatting in a rough circle around the campfire.

The fire showed red flame and threw out a welcome warmth as he went forward. There were six men there and they turned to stare at him with inquisitive eyes. None of them looked like the two men he had spotted earlier that morning.

One of the men asked quickly: 'You the new hand that Saunders hired a week or so ago?'

'That's right.' Bart went down on to his haunches, held his hands out to the fire. He spoke easily and quietly. 'He sent me out here this morning, but he only mentioned two hands being here.' He looked around the circle of faces. 'Could be that he made a mistake.'

'No mistake, feller,' grunted a tall, lean-faced man on the other side of the fire. 'Me and the boys brought over a herd from the other side of the range.' He snickered thinly and there was something evil on his scarred face that sent a shiver through Bart.

'Sure,' muttered another man thinly. 'The other side of the range. The Benson side.' He laughed harshly, and eased the gun from his holster, sliding it smoothly back with a reflex gesture.

Bart nodded. 'Heard a lot about that feller Benson,' he said. He was figuring on none of these men knowing that he had been the one who had found the dead man. Out on the range, the men would be away from the ranch for several weeks at a time and although it was a risk, he figured it was a good one. 'What happened to him? Did hear that he'd been makin' trouble for Jeb Saunders.'

The scar-faced man spat into the fire. 'He always was a troublemaker, that one. Came from somewheres up north so maybe that had somethin' to do with it. Kept damming the water supply down the hills. We lost some cattle, then the boss decided to do somethin' about it.'

'Know who killed him?' Deliberately, Bart stared into the fire as he spoke, then pulled out a piece of meat from the pan. There was no expression on his face or in his voice.

The other sat where he was, never taking his eyes off Bart. Then he said thinly: 'You ask a lot of questions, feller. You got any interest in this deal?'

'Some,' Bart, watching the other with his head hunched forward on his shoulders, his eyes never wavering, felt sure that the man knew what was coming. 'I work for Saunders now. I think I ought to know where I stand in this deal, I ought to know who my enemies are, especially in town.'

'So long as you stay in with Saunders, they won't dare shoot you in the back. Only Benson might have had the guts to do that and he's dead. There's nobody else.'

Another man laughed thinly at that. His scowl was one of grim, sardonic amusement. 'Reckon Wiley ought to know about that, eh, Wiley?'

The man with the scar twitched his lips into a travesty of a grin. 'I sure hope that the Benson gal don't agree to sell to Saunders. I had a score myself to settle with Benson. Now he's dead, I'll have to do it with his kin. I say we ought to burn the ranch down about 'em. That ranch foreman, Jed Clayton, can still cause us some trouble. We ought to have shot him when we had the chance.'

Quiet fell again around the circle of men. Bart ate slowly, feeling the eyes of the others on him, appraising him, trying to figure him out. In particular, he knew that

Wiley was watching him closely. The man's face had been familiar when he had first seen him, but he had been unable to put a name to it until the other cowhand had mentioned it in passing. Ed Wiley, a notorious killer from way back east. A couple of years before, the posses of more than a dozen towns had ridden out after him and his gang, but although they had caught up with most of his men and strung them up on the outskirts of the towns, or buried them in Boot Hill, they had never found Ed Wiley himself. Now he had turned up here. More than ever before, Bart wondered what he had let himself in for, riding into this place like this, alone, with only his guns to keep him alive. It seemed as though Jeb Saunders could call on the services of every notorious gunslinger in the State. He shifted his position slightly, moving a little way back from the fire so that he could keep an eye on all of the men. One of the men brought a bottle of rye from his saddlebag and passed it round. When it was empty, he got another. Bart drank his share and continued to watch. A couple of the men simply got silly. The older men like Ed Wiley never batted an eyelid. It was dark now and the stars were out in their thousands. There was a stillness over the range and it was so quiet that Bart could hear the cattle moving around contentedly in the grass. The fire began to die down and two of the men went after more wood.

Presently, Bart rose, went over to the sorrel and pulled down his blanket roll. The others watched him, but said nothing. They were still unsure of him, still disinclined to talk in front of him. He unrolled the blanket a little distance from the fire, then lay down in it. After a while, he fell asleep and did not wake until the morning.

For two days, he worked the range with the other cowboys, herding the steers, repairing the fences wherever they had been broken down. The men talked little about Jeb Saunders or about the Benson affair and after a while, he reached the conclusion that Ed Wiley had been talking to them, warning them in no uncertain terms against giving him any information. Then, on the third day, word came that he was to go back to the ranch. He had the feeling that trouble of some kind was due to break out pretty soon. Maybe this was it, he thought grimly, as he swung into the saddle and hit the trail.

None of his movements had haste but all of them counted. He looked back for a moment, over his shoulder, at the camp. He hadn't seen Ed Wiley for almost a day and wondered vaguely whether the other had ridden on ahead of him. Maybe Jeb Saunders was still intent on taking no chances. Maybe he knew about Reva Benson talking to him and there would be another drygulcher waiting for him somewhere along to trail back to the ranch. Only this time, with a man like Wiley, a professional killer, he would need all of his senses alert if he was to get past him alive.

He found his way downward through the pines and on to the lower trail which wound its way through the middle of the wide valley. Down here, he would make a far better target for a man with a high-powered rifle who could hit him from a distance, but he was relying on Wiley wanting to use his sixes and along the lower trail, there would be less chance of him being able to strike out of ambush. He had made his choice then and he got to the level within an hour, giving the sorrel its head. Here and there, in the very middle of the valley, the ground was rough and uneven; a broken land of tree stumps which thrust themselves up out of the stony earth, of shadowy coulees and tufted-grass openness. He knew that if Wiley were there, crouched somewhere along the higher trail, he would have spotted him by now, was possibly riding parallel with him, biding his time, playing a cat-and-mouse game with him.

The realization heightened the tension which had been riding him ever since he had left camp. How much did Jeb

Saunders suspect about him? Possibly only a little but with a man in his position, the life of one man meant little if it afforded him a continuation of the security upon which everything he owned rested.

By noon, he was still in open rangeland, but the hills to the north came crowding in a little closer and up ahead, where the creek splashed down through the pines, they approached to within a quarter of a mile of the trail. It was here, he figured, that Wiley would make his play, if he made it at all. Carefully, he loosened the irons in their holsters, sitting easily in the saddle, outwardly calm, but with every nerve and muscle stretched to the utmost limit of tautness.

Unobtrusively, he turned the sorrel slightly so that he would not be squinting into the sun when he approached the bend in the trail. If things panned out right as far as Wiley was concerned, it might serve to force Saunders' hand. He didn't want to bank on it, but it would possibly be the only time the other made a mistake and he wanted to be around when it happened. If Wiley made an attempt to shoot him from cover, then it would be simply that Jeb Saunders had ordered the killing. Professional gunslinger though he was, Ed Wiley was still in the other man's pay and he would carry out his orders to the letter if he knew what was good for him.

Bart had the feeling that even if he hated him as much as the look in his eyes had shown the first time they had met, he would not jump him from cover just to satisfy that hatred, unless Jeb Saunders had given the order, had said that Bart Nolan was getting too nosey to remain alive.

Wiley made his play the moment the sorrel turned the bend and reached the point where the trail was closest to the trees. He was crouched somewhere in the underbrush, out of sight, but Bart caught the flash of his sixes as he fired and his actions were swift and instinctive. His mood, as he slipped sideways in the saddle was both suddenly reckless and impatient, tinged with a faint anger that had been boiling up since he had realized the danger he was in. His guns cleared leather in a savage, lightning movement, spitting flame in the same moment. There came another shot from the brush that went wide, then there was silence. Dropping from the saddle, Bart went forward on foot, moving carefully now. When he found Ed Wiley, he knew that he needn't have bothered with caution. The gunslinger was dead. Both of Bart's bullets had found their mark in spite of the fact that he had been sliding from the saddle when he had fired.

One had made a neat hole in the other's chest, just right of the breastbone. The other had hit him higher up in the left shoulder. The second might have incapacitated Wiley, causing him to miss with his third shot. But the other had killed him outright, cutting off his life in a single red-edged instant.

Bart looked about him for any sign of other men in the brush, but after a few moments he was satisfied that Wiley had been alone. He had been so sure, so confident of his own ability to shoot down a man from ambush that the thought of failure had never even entered his head. Bart walked back to his horse and mounted slowly. He was hungry and he needed rest. He could feel the toll of that long ride in the hot sun, with the threat of sudden death hanging over him and the sudden let-down from the tension washed through his body.

He stopped by the creek and ate. The sun passed its zenith and began sliding slowly down the cloudless sky to the west. Jerking round the sorrel's head, he moved along the trail again. If he was to reach the ranch before nightfall, he would have to make up for lost time. That night, he intended to have a long over-due talk with Jeb Saunders. There were lights beginning to show in the windows of the ranch-house as he rode down the trail through the blue-grass meadows from the low hills. He saw them from a distance just as night was beginning to deepen over the mountains in the far distance, where they stood out with a deep purple flush against the skyline. He could make out one or two of the cowhands near the bunkhouse and there was a small bunch of horses in the corral. As he rode in, he was acutely aware of several of the hired hands watching him closely.

A moment or two later, the door of the ranch burst open and Saunders stalked out into the courtyard. He stood for a moment, straddle-legged, staring up at Bart as if seeing a ghost, then he caught himself and motioned the other down. 'Glad you managed to get here, Nolan,' he said, forcing a grin. 'You look as though you've had some kinda trouble on the trail. Nothin' happened, I trust.' There was no concern in his voice. It was that of a man who was sorely puzzled and wanted to find out everything he could without giving himself away.

Bart smiled bitterly as he dismounted. 'There was trouble,' he admitted, 'but it weren't nothin' I couldn't handle. Somebody tried to drygulch me on the way back. Shot at me from the scrub.'

'You see who it was?' inquired Saunders sharply. His eyes were narrowed to mere slits under the heavy, black brows.

'Sure did.' Bart watched the expression on the other's face closely. 'He's back there now if you want to go out and git him. Name's Ed Wiley. I'd call him a professional killer, but seeing that you hired him, Mister Saunders, maybe you know a little more about him than I do.'

The other shook his head ponderously. He seemed to have regained control of himself. 'I just hired him as an extra hand.' he said heavily. 'I never figgered he'd turn out bad like that. You'd better come inside, though, Nolan. There's something we have to talk about.'

THREE

THE LONG ROPE

A fragrant smell of tobacco hit Bart as he followed Saunders inside the ranch. The room itself was tastefully furnished, as he guessed it would be, decorated in the heavy Southern style. The other man's eyes were like flint arrowheads as he seated himself behind the large, rolltop desk and motioned Bart to the chair in front of it.

With an effort, Bart forced his mind back to reality. This was the first time that it had struck him forcibly how a man such as Saunders might live. He seated himself carefully in the chair, suddenly unsure of himself. There was something in the other's gaze that he didn't like.

Jeb Saunders spoke up sharply: 'I've been watchin' you closely, Nolan, ever since you joined my outfit. You looked like a man who knew how to handle himself and didn't ask too many questions. That kind of man I like. But recently, I've had cause to change my mind about you. Every other man in the Lazy V outfit comes to me with his background well known. Maybe he's a professional killer like Ed Wiley, but his past means nothin' to me so long as he does as he's told and keeps his nose clean as far as I'm concerned.'

Bart stared at the other intently, trying to penetrate the

mask of expressionless calm which covered his face. The other suspected something. He felt sure of that. But try as he would, he could not make up his mind definitely how much it was.

'If there's somethin' on your mind, I reckon it might be best if you told me now.' He shrugged. 'Mebbe there was trouble somewhere in your past. But I own the law out here so there's no need to git your dander up about Sheriff Foley in Nashville. He'll do exactly as I tell him.' The grey eyes swept over Bart in a swift, weighing glance. 'As for the shooting of Ed Wiley. Well, if he did shoot at you from cover, then it was self-defence and that ain't a hanging crime anywheres in the State. You know that.'

'Seems to me that you've got quite a lot of explainin' to do, Mister Saunders,' said Bart quietly. He never removed his steady gaze from the other's face for a single instant, saw the man's face swell up and flush heavily. 'Ed Wiley was workin' for you. He obeyed your orders and the way I figger it, he wouldn't shoot me unless you told him to.'

The other thinned his lips. 'You accusing me of trying to get you killed, Nolan?' he gritted sharply. His red face choked fiery with anger. His big hands reached out and gripped the top of the desk convulsively and he half-rose to his feet, a muscle jumping in his cheek.

'That's the way I see it, Saunders.' Bart knew the moment when the chips were down, ready to be raked in; it always held a sense of both fulfilment and danger.

'You're making a big mistake, Nolan.' There was anger and a grim tightness in the other's tone. 'You can't talk to me like that, you know! I've had men shot for less than that.'

'Just as I figgered,' replied Bart calmly. 'Seems to me that someone has been spreadin' it around town that I killed old man Benson. You're the only man who would do that. Nobody else in Nashville knows anythin' about me except for the sheriff and there's no call for him to do anythin' like that.'

Jeb Saunders flinched as though the words had touched a sore spot. He leaned heavily back in his chair, clearly fighting for control of himself. Bart guessed that there would be a gun tucked away in the top drawer of the desk but the other was too careful a man to make a play for it, knowing that he would be dead before he even got the drawer open. Bart smiled grimly to himself. It must have come as a big shock to Saunders to learn that Ed Wiley, one of the fastest gunhawks in that part of the country had been outdrawn and killed, even when shooting from cover. It would give Saunders pause before he tried to go for his own gun. He might do his level best to shoot Bart in the back, but he would never take the risk of gunning for him in fair fight.

For a long moment, the grey eyes stared into his own, filled with a murderous hate. Then Saunders forced himself to relax and an oily grin spread itself over his thick, coarse features. His cruel, strong lips flattened themselves over his teeth and he breathed a long, deep sigh. 'I've no call to fight with you, Nolan,' he said finally, forcing evenness into his deep voice. 'But I can't keep you on my payroll any longer. You realize that, of course. Whatever their pasts might be there is one thing I demand from a man above everything else. Loyalty to me.'

'And I haven't been loyal. Is that it?' demanded Bart. The tension was relaxing a little and he knew, with some kind of instinct deep within him, that there was nothing to fear from the other at the moment. He would still make sure that he never left the town alive, but death would come for Bart Nolan at some time in the future, probably from the gun of one of Jeb's other hired hands.

Saunders spread his hands wide on the top of the desk. His voice quivered a little as he said thinly: 'You know the kind of men I have to hire to keep law and order around these parts, Nolan. With men like that, I can't afford to take any chances. Pretty soon, I shall have the largest spread in the whole State. Louisiana is wide open at the moment and I aim to grab myself the biggest piece of it – and nobody is going to stand in my way. Nobody, get me?'

Bart grinned tightly. He said goadingly. 'You ain't God, you know, Mister Saunders. This ain't 1783. You'll soon have the whole state of Louisiana to contend with and you can't fight them. The whole country is on the move westwards. The settlers will be headin' this way soon in their thousands, some for California and the others may settle here.'

'They won't get the chance, Nolan.' Something infernal seemed to have gotten into the other, or maybe, thought Bart, it had been there all of the time and was only just beginning to come out. 'I'm the law around here and there's nobody who's going to say any different.'

'You can't stand in the way of progress.' Bart shook his head. 'The war's been finished for close on six years now. The country will start rebuilding. You and your kind will find yourselves at the end of a rope if you aren't careful.'

For a moment, he figured that the other was going to make a try for the gun in the desk and take the chance of outdrawing him. The fury in Saunders' eyes was plain to see. Under the shaggy black brows they were filled with a virulence Bart had never seen before.

Then he sank back in his chair, keeping his hands on the desk. 'Just where do you fit in with the Benson girl?' he asked abruptly. 'Two of my men spotted them on my territory and went up to move them off. Seems you were having quite a parley with 'em:'

'So that's why you ordered Ed Wiley to take care of me along the trail?'

'Could be. But now that you're here, I reckon I'd better

hear about it from you. If you're thinking of throwing in your hand with them, I'd advise you against it. Once Reva Benson sells out to me, I'll own every spread around Nashville. Those who ain't for me, will be against me then.'

'You figger that you can get away with murder every time?'

Saunders said slowly, carefully, 'There ain't nobody to stop me, Nolan. Like I said, I'm the law here. If you're wise, you'll remember that. I've got a good memory and you'll pay for these idle threats you've made against me tonight. Believe me, you'll pay.'

Bart chuckled mirthlessly. 'You figgerin' on having me shot in the back as I ride away, Saunders?'

The other shrugged. He was completely on balance again, master of the situation. 'No cause for that,' he said easily, the eyes still hard and narrowed. 'You can't get out of Nashville without me knowing your every move.'

Bart sat quite still and mulled things over in his mind, careful not to let any expression show through on to his face. He was aware that all the time he had been speaking, the other had been watching him closely. He knew that he wouldn't have much chance to get away and there would be no point in trying to send a message from the telegraph office. And once in Nashville, they would have his back full of bullets before he could cause any further trouble. But he had to go through with this now that he had started. He only hoped that he hadn't overplayed his hand.

Saunders got to his feet and stood for a moment, looking down at him. He said tightly. 'You made a mistake when you met the Benson girl on my range, Nolan. There's something about you that I don't like. You've got the look of the killer breed to you, but I don't know anything about you like I do the others. For that reason, I figger that you could be dangerous.'

Bart got to his feet and tension filled his chest. The

48

other wouldn't shoot him here close to the ranch. That might be asking for trouble. Saunders still had some enemies in Nashville. No, he'd have him killed well away from the ranch, probably in Nashville itself where Sheriff Foley stood behind the tin star and meted out justice.

'It's getting dark,' said Saunders thinly. 'You'd better start now, amigo. It's a long ride into Nashville at night. Be careful. There are cut-throats in these parts and I can't answer for your safety once you leave my ranch.' The smile seemed to have been painted on his face, but it never touched the hard grey eyes.

Outside, in the warm darkness, Bart stepped up to leather and sat easily in the saddle for a long moment, listening. He could see nobody in the darkness and guessed that the rest of the men were in the bunkhouse or the cookshack. He waited a little longer. There might be someone waiting in the shadows, with a six-gun or a rifle trained on him at that moment. Behind him, Saunders might have yielded to the fury in him and was preparing to use the gun in the desk. But he had diced with chance too many times in the past and had grown contemptuous of it. He pulled the sorrel's head around and rode away from the ranch. The moon was up, edging over the tops of the mulberry trees over by the cookshack as he walked the sorrel back along the gentle rise. Having just come in from the trail, there was nothing of his left in the bunkhouse. His roll was tied securely to the saddle. He turned right and rode quietly through the night. The grass underfoot was still green and made very little noise as the sorrel pushed its feet through it, moving easily. He reached the narrow tributary of the creek where it flowed past the front of the ranch and put the sorrel to the water, splashing along the stream for a hundred yards or so before coming out on the opposite bank. On the other side, he stopped, thinking. Saunders would expect him to be a little panicky after what he had said, would expect him to hit the trail and keep on riding fast for Nashville, or if he were clever and wanted to escape, to even head in the opposite direction, hoping to be well clear of the area by dawn. There would be men watching both trails.

He sat the sorrel in the dark for some time, but apart from the bullfrogs croaking hoarsely in the water and the fireflies which darted and flickered in front of him, there was no other sound in the stillness. Whatever intentions Saunders might have towards him, it would wait until morning, he decided, unless he tried to make a break for it across country, out into the desertlands to the south and west.

He gave the horse its head and rode due east through the trees, in the yellow moonlight, finding his way downwards through the tall pines, following the narrow trail which was slippery and treacherous with a carpeting of pine needles. The sorrel made a silent passage on this thick and spongy trail, picking its way sure-footedly in the dimness. He paused at intervals to let the horse blow and it was at these times that he listened again, straining his ears to pick out the slightest sounds. Once, he thought that he heard the sound of horses and voices, faint in the distance, but he couldn't be sure. Whoever had been riding that way, must have turned and headed back again.

A little before he struck level ground again, he broke free of the shrouding woodland and sat for a moment looking down into the valley. There were another two miles to go yet before he hit the boundary fence of the Saunders' spread. If he'd judged Jeb Saunders right, he figured that they wouldn't try to silence him until he had crossed the fence. Then they could claim no knowledge of how he had been killed, or by whom. Straining his eyes, he sought for a pattern in the shifting lines of shadow below, that lay spread out in the flooding moonlight. When he thought that he had found one, when he knew exactly where he was, he put his spurs to the weary sorrel once more and rode on, avoiding the open patches of moonlight whenever he could.

The narrow trail made a silver ribbon through the pines as he approached the fence. Half a mile from it, he had the sensation of riders all around him, although he could see nothing. Then he heard one of them coming along and moved the sorrel into the trees, holding his hand clamped over the animal's nostrils.

The rider approached along the trail, moving cautiously. In the moonlight, it was just possible for Bart to make out the hawk-like features beneath the wide-brimmed hat pulled low over his eyes and the sixes slung low. The man rode warily, but there was no fear in him and his gaze kept flicking from side to side. Here, thought Bart, was one of the hunters.

He remained hidden among the trees until the sound of the other man's mount had faded into the distance. Then he quit his hiding place and dipped down along the trees in the direction from which the man had come. The word had gone out, without a doubt, that Nolan was no longer in favour with Saunders and he was to be stopped from talking, just in case he knew anything important. Bart smiled grimly to himself in the moonlight. That was the big trouble as far as he was concerned. He knew so very little about this man who had set himself up as self-styled king of Nashville. That he was the man behind several of the recent slayings, he knew. But holding the law in the palm of his hand as he did, it would be impossible to get a conviction against him on those charges; besides it was doubtful if he had ever actually pulled the trigger himself, except perhaps, in the case of Joel Benson; and none of the killers in his pay were going to talk to the law.

51

Saunders had been very clever in that respect, choosing men whose pasts were such that they would never dare testify against him.

But there was something in the man's past which would bear checking, something which would explain the sudden and spectacular change in fortunes. It could be that he had made something on the sale of beef to the Confederates, but Bart had the feeling, deep down inside, that it was something more than that. Something that Saunders kept so well hidden that it wasn't going to be easy prying it loose from the past.

He hit the range wire, stretched out across the trail, loosened it and went through, closing it down behind him. Now he was on his own, unable to get any word out of Nashville, unable to ask for help from the Rangers Office or from the office of the U.S. Marshal.

He continued to ride while the moon slipped down behind the western hills and the darkness which always seemed to come before the dawn lay over the land. As soon as the dawn showed red, he rode out into the open before Nashville, coming out boldly into the openness. In the first flush of dawn, with the dew sparkling on the blue grass and the country around him empty of riders, the night seemed like something dark and unreal, soon forgotten.

At noon, he rode into Nashville. Behind him, lay a long, dusty trail which stretched all the way back to the Saunders ranch, back to that threat of death. Even before he reached the town, he passed through a cluster of wooden huts which had been hastily thrown up on the outskirts. Here, too, he rode through a sea of tents with the acrid smoke of cooking fire rising up into the still, shimmering air which hung heavy over the land. The settlers were beginning to arrive already, but he doubted whether any of them would get a fair shake from Saunders. They would be lucky if they managed to stay alive for a month. But soon, if they continued to come in, they would be a force to be reckoned with, they might be made to band together and stand up to crooks like Jeb Saunders and his hired killers.

The town still had that waiting silence hanging over it which he had noticed when he had first ridden into it from the opposite direction with Joel Benson's dead and ravaged body lying across his saddle. There were few people on the streets and those who sat on the wooden sidewalks seemed to eye him with a new kind of respect. He guessed that, as yet, word had not come in that Jeb Saunders wanted him dead.

He rode directly to the solitary hotel, halfway along the main street and unsaddled after hitching the sorrel to the rail. He took down his saddlebag and walked to the board-walk in front of the hotel, throwing a quick look around him before pushing open the doors and walking inside. The long gallery fronting the hotel held a few wooden chairs and most of these were occupied by a motley crew of gunmen and men with the tin stars of lawmen pinned on to their shirts. He didn't doubt that all of these men owed their allegience to Jeb Saunders.

Inside the long hallway he paused. He knew that he ought to feel something at a moment such as this, when the decision to fight had been made and the die had been cast – something of expectation, or fear or uncertainty. But there was nothing like that in his mind or his body, only a vague and empty weariness. He had been on the trail far too long without any sleep. His thinking was lax and it seemed to be just a luxury to be off-saddle and standing.

Crossing the wide lobby, he approached the desk. The clerk was a small, thin-faced man who stared up at him through thick-lensed spectacles, like a scared jack-rabbit.

'Got a room for a few days?' demanded Bart.

'Sure, sure.' The other spun the register and handed him the pen. 'You intending to stay here long, stranger?'

'Just a few days until I've cleared up some unfinished business.' He stood for a moment with the pen poised over the book, scanning the names in the register. The one scrawled above his own was that of Jess Ordway. Bart clamped his lips tight. So Ordway was in the hotel, probably waiting for him. It said a lot for the hold that Saunders had over this town, that a vicious, wanted killer such as that could come in here and sign his name quite openly in the hotel register.

He signed his own name with a flourish, then looked up with his lips quirking. 'Seems like I've heard of that feller there,' he said quietly, pointing with the pen at the name over his own. 'How come he's still around here. I heard he was wanted by every lawman in the State.'

The clerk looked scared for a moment and his Adam's apple bobbed up and down nervously as he said huskily: 'We got ourselves a sheriff in Nashville who don't see a lot of things like that.' He looked about him as he spoke, as if frightened of being overheard.

'Sheriff Foley. Yeah, I've heard of him,' Bart nodded, threw the other a swift glance. 'Know anything about a man called Saunders? Jeb Saunders?'

The clerk at once turned guarded. 'Sure, he has a spread outa town, to the west. What you want to know about him fer?' He had a weak face and his eyes never seemed to meet the other man's. 'You don't want to go tangling with him, stranger. He's too big a man for that. You's only be getting yourself into trouble, big trouble.'

'I figger I can take care of myself,' Bart replied. He guessed that the other was so scared he would give away nothing of importance about Jeb Saunders. Besides if he started asking too many questions at this point, somebody would be sure to drop the word to Sheriff Foley and he would find himself inside the County jail with no chance to do anything. He took the key which the other tendered and went up the stairs to his room which was right at the very top.

Raising the window, he glanced down into the dusty street. He could see nobody who seemed to be taking more than a natural interest in the hotel and guessed that either Saunders' men had not yet reached town, or the other had decided to hold his hand for a little while, knowing that he couldn't get away, and possibly anxious to know what his next move would be. Saunders was a careful man. He wouldn't want him dead before he found out just who, and what, he was.

After washing the dust of the trail from himself, he lay down on the bed by the window and allowed some of the weariness to quit his body. Outside, the sun was hot and the street remained empty. After an hour or so, he went down into the hotel dining room and had his lunch. There were few visitors at the tables and he saw no sign of Jess Ordway. He recognized the sheriff in one corner, but the other paid him no attention.

Finishing his meal, he fashioned himself a quirly, and went outside on to the boardwalk. The air was cooler now and Nashville a little livelier than when he had ridden in that morning. He checked that the sorrel was being cared for at the local livery stables, then headed for the sheriff's office. There were things he wanted to find out before he went any further.

The sheriff looked up in surprise as he pushed open the doors and went inside. Then a curious look spread over his face and he started to his feet.

'Better sit right where you are, Sheriff, until you've heard me out,' said Bart with a dangerous glint in his eyes. His hands hovered close to the irons in their holsters. 'I don't want to have to shoot down a rattler like you in cold blood but I might have to do it if you force my hand. This is my play for the moment, so just you sit back and relax.'

The lawman glared at him for a moment, threw a swift glance over Bart's shoulders towards the door, then shrugged his shoulders resignedly.

'Speak your piece, stranger,' he said through thinned lips. 'But I reckon I ought to warn you that there's been word from Jeb Saunders that you killed a man back there on his territory. He's considerin' swearing out a charge of murder against you.'

'Just what I figgered he might do,' muttered Bart calmly. He toyed with the gun in his right holster for a moment, saw the beads of sweat pop out on the lawman's forehead and the look of fear which sprang momentarily into his eyes. The other was scared and Bart wondered if it might be possible to get the other to talk.

'That rattler I killed back there drygulched me on the trail as I was ridin' back to the ranch,' he said harshly, 'but there were no witnesses and I guess that in this town, Saunders' word is law. But I didn't come here to talk about a killer like Ed Wiley. I want to know somethin' of the Benson spread.'

The sheriff licked his lips nervously. 'Benson?' he said throatily. 'He's dead. You brung him in yourself.' His eyes became cunning. 'Point of fact, stranger, there is word goin' around that you killed him, shot him in the back and robbed him.'

Bart smiled grimly. 'I can guess who started that rumour, sheriff. Only you don't even believe it yourself.'

'Who says I don't?' snapped the other. A worried frown etched itself deep between his eyes. He was puzzled. Maybe, figured Bart, the other had pinned him as an ordinary killer, hired in the normal way by Jeb Saunders and then shrugged off and declared dangerous, when he knew too much.

'Because if I killed and robbed him, as you're sayin', why should I whip him before shooting him in the back? There's only one man who hated Joel Benson enough to do somethin' like that. Jeb Saunders!'

'He's got an alibi that'll stick in any court,' said the other grimly. 'You'll never make that charge stick.'

'I'll bet he has.' Anger thinned Bart's tone. He saw the sweat running freely down the other's face and it gave him a savage feeling of delight. 'Where's Jeb's hired killer?'

'I don't know who you mean.' The other's throat worked convulsively for a moment.

'Jess Ordway. He's in town somewhere, probably coming gunning for me. I asked you where he is. I won't ask again.'

'How should I know?'

'Because you're in cahoots with Jeb Saunders yourself,' snarled Bart. 'You can make a good guess as to what he's going to do and when he'll make his play. You'll have had your instructions by now from Saunders. Think hard – and it had better be good.'

Foley said, without putting any real force behind it, 'You lookin' for trouble, Nolan? Ordway's a bad man to tangle with.'

'So I hear.' If he was surprised by the other's sudden change of attitude, he was careful not to show it. The sheriff's face was tight and tense. 'Now are you going to tell me where he is, or do I have to beat it outa you?'

'You're bluffin', Nolan,' muttered the other, but he was beginning to bluster. 'You wouldn't dare attack me. Saunders will have your hide for this.'

'Mebbe so. But you won't be alive to see it.' Bart hooked his thumbs in his gunbelt and moved slowly towards the other.

Foley moistened his lips again, looked about him frantically like a cornered rat. Then he started talking, the words spilling from his lips. Maybe he figured that Bart wouldn't remain alive long after he met up with Ordway. Maybe he figured that this was the way that Saunders had planned it. But whatever his reason, even if it was only the human one of wanting to stay alive, he talked.

'He rode into town before dawn. Put up at the hotel and then left. The last I saw of him, he was headed towards the saloon. I guess you'll find him there playing cards.'

'That's better,' Bart nodded. 'Now you're showing some sense, lawman.' There was a disgusted tone to his voice which the sheriff couldn't help noticing. He removed his hands from his belt and stopped by the window, glancing out. The street was still almost deserted. A few cowpokes could be seen along the broadwalks, and here and there, he noticed one or two of the settlers. Across the street, was the saloon, next door to the Stage Office.

The bat-wing doors were shut but the place was open for business as usual.

He swung back on the sheriff. The hard look was back in his eyes. The frightened eyes searched his for a moment, flicked away and down to the ground.

'You goin' after Ordway now, Nolan?'

Bart gave the other a long, cool glance. 'Not yet. I haven't finished with you, Sheriff. Since I figger you know I didn't kill Benson, who do you reckon did it? Saunders or one of his hired killers?' He raised his eyebrows. 'Well'?'

All of the fight seemed to have been knocked out of the other, but he still shook his head. 'If you didn't kill him, I don't know who did. There's plenty in Nashville who'll swear that you did shoot him in the back and brung him back here to throw suspicion off yourself and on to Saunders. Why don't you play it smart and get outa town while you have the chance?'

Bart grinned thinly. 'And have a couple of Saunders' men jump me on the trail outside Nashville? That's what he's hoping I'll do.'

'Then what more do you want to know?' The uneasiness was back in Foley's voice, but there was something else there too and Bart tried hard to place it. A growing sense of confidence, perhaps? He could be stalling for time, hoping that either Saunders or one of his killers would happen along and force the issue.

Very gently, Bart eased one of his long-barrelled Peacemakers from its holster and hefted it into his hand. The sweat started out on the other's face again and he backed away. 'You're not going to shoot me down like that – in cold blood.' His voice was suddenly frantic with fear.

'I've got no feelin' about shooting a rat like you, Foley,' gritted Bart. 'But I asked you about the Benson affair. What's goin' to happen if Reva Benson refuses to sell out to Saunders?'

'I don't know!'

There was no time to do this thing as he would have liked. Bart's left wrist clenched and he swung it hard at the other's face. It scraped down the side of his cheek, drawing blood and the lawman fell back against the table, knocking it over with his weight as he went down. With an effort, he lurched to his feet, dabbing at his face, keeping his hands away from the guns in his belt. He came slowly upright, thick lips sneering. 'You'll pay for that when Saunders is through with you, Nolan,' he grated. 'I reckon he's going to like this a heap.'

'Saunders can go to blazes as far as I'm concerned.' Bart said thinly. 'I don't stand for any backshooting like what happened to Benson, particularly when some polecat tries to pin the blame for the murder on me. I ought to shoot you as you stand. But you're going to talk and talk fast. And don't think that any of your friends can help you. Remember that you'll be the first to get a bullet if they try to break in on us.'

Bart saw the sudden look of fear which leapt again into

the sheriff's eyes and knew that the other had been depending on such a thing happening. It had probably never struck him that he would be dead the second anyone tried to force their way into the office. He licked his lips, swallowed, then said in a hoarse, grating voice: 'Saunders is planning to fire the ranch if she don't agree to sell, at his price, by tomorrow night. He means to have that spread and nobody's goin' to stand in his way. You'll be a goddarned fool if you try.'

'What about Benson himself? Did Saunders kill him?'

'I don't know. He may have. He doesn't tell me everything. It could have been one of his boys acting on his orders. I was told that you had done it and that if you showed up here you were to be put under arrest.'

Bart nodded. He felt sure now that the other was telling the truth. He had no cause to lie. Jess Ordway was known to be one of the fastest guns north of the Rio and as far as Foley was concerned, Bart Nolan would be dead before sundown and Jeb Saunders would know nothing of this little talk.

'What about Saunders himself? You know anything about him? Where he got all of that money to start his spread again after the war finished?'

Again there was that shifting glance before the sheriff looked back at him. 'You're playing a smart game, Nolan, but you're not half as smart as you think. If there's anything like that in his past, you're not likely to find it and I know nothin' about it.'

Bart's features were flat, bereft of all emotion. He holstered his gun easily but kept his hand palmed over it as it rested in the leather. The sheriff moved a little to one side as he read the killing look in Bart's eyes. 'I don't know anything more about Jeb Saunders. I swear I don't.'

Bart shrugged. His face showed nothing as he went on calmly. 'I guess that's a pity, Foley.' He smiled thinly at the lawman. With a swift motion, he lunged over the desk and grabbed the other by his shirt, pulling him hard across the mahogany, jerking him upright. 'If there's anythin' I really hate, Foley, it's a crooked lawman, a two-timing sheriff. I reckon I ought to kill you here and now, to save myself the trouble of having to do it later. But you might be of some use in the future.'

'You're talking crazy now, Nolan!' The other's voice was shrill and high-pitched. His features were stiff as he stared up into Bart's eyes. 'Do you reckon you're going to get out of Nashville alive?' His voice tapered off as Bart smiled at him again.

'If I don't, then by God, I'm going to take a lot of crooked polecats with me,' snarled the other. 'But first, I'd better take good care of you. I don't want you running to Saunders and blabbing about this little talk we've had.'

Foley's eyes flickered faintly. Then, with a sudden, swift motion which almost took Bart by surprise, his hand flashed down, reaching for the guns in his belt. At the same moment, he lurched backward, the chair behind him crashing to the floor as he clawed for his irons. Savagely, instinctively, Bart lashed out with his right hand. There was no time to go for his gun, no time for a killing shot with the bulk of the heavy desk standing in the way. His clenched fist caught the other on the side of the head as he swayed back, stunning him for a moment. Then, bracing himself, Bart moved in, driving forward around the side of the desk, grabbing for the sheriff's wrist, forcing it downward so that he would be unable to fire a killing shot. The other struggled desperately before he was forced to unclench his fingers from around the gun, as Bart threatened to snap his wrist with the intense pressure he was applying.

Savagely, fighting for his life, the sheriff twisted, surged under Bart with a heave of almost superhuman strength,

61

hurling him back against the desk. The edge of it caught Bart in the small of the back and a stab of agony shot through his body. Swiftly, he reared up, got the other's wrist in his grip once more and brought it down hard on the side of the desk. He heard the bone crack, but he was furious with pain. Lashing out with his foot, he caught Foley on the side of the shin, sending him staggering. All the time, the other had not uttered a single cry for help. Following up the kick with fists, elbows and knees, he drove the other back to the wall, threw a solid right jab to the man's heart, and finished it with a savage, breath-stopping left to the jaw. The sheriff went down as if pole-axed, doubled over, his eyes glazing over. Bart gave him one last battering with both fists, stood breathing harshly for a moment, then picked up the other and dragged him over to the steel bars of the cells. The sheriff was groaning softly deep in his throat as Bart located the keys, opened one of the cells and thrust the other inside. Locking the door again, he tossed the keys on to the floor in one corner and went out into the street.

Somewhere in Nashville, Jess Ordway was waiting to gun him down, He forced himself to breathe more slowly. He had heard of Ordway from way back. A born killer with a reputation that stretched over half a dozen States. A man who prided himself on being the fastest draw in the State; but also a man who knew he had to live up to his reputation. He would gun Bart down in front of witnesses, knowing that whatever happend, it would be a case of self-defence now that he was in Saunders' employ. And those witnesses would see to it that it was a fair fight, as fair as men like Ordway ever fought.

Bart's lips twisted into a thin smile. At least, he doubted if the gunslinger would shoot him in the back, or from ambush as Ed Wiley had tried to kill him. He might have a few friends with him, inside the saloon, placed discreetly among the other men, ready to back his play if necessary.

There was still a brief, occasional stab of pain in the small of his back as he walked slowly along the wide, empty street, but he forced himself to ignore it, flexing his hands slowly like a boxer as he paced the dust. Where was Ordway now? he wondered. Standing behind those bat-wing doors with his guns in his hands, or waiting at the bar or gambling tables for him to make his play? Ordway, he recalled, was a man who always liked a touch of drama with his killings. How many men he had killed in gunplay, Bart didn't know; and the man had some stake to his repu-tation, evil though it was.

Easing the Peacemakers in their holsters, he paced forward slowly towards the doors of the saloon. From inside, he heard the sound of music. Someone was playing the old piano as if his life depended upon it. Probably, he thought grimly, Ordway had his gun on the pianist.

Aware that he was taking his life in his hands, alert for the slightest movement, the faintest sound that could mean trouble, he crossed the street. The soft shush of his feet in the dust was the only sound that accompanied him. He reached the doors, hesitated for a moment, then pushed them open and stepped inside the saloon. The music stopped on a jangling discord. For a moment, he was aware of the men at the bar watching him, then his gaze switched away to where Ordway sat with his back to him at one of the card tables.

FOUR

SHAKEDOWN

Bart deliberately checked himself as he stood in the doorway, feeling the touch of the swinging doors on his back as they closed behind him. For a tense moment, it was as if all sound inside the saloon had been sheared off by a machete. Behind the bar, he saw the flash of mirrors and grew aware that Ordway's face, reflected in them as he sat at the table, was fixed intently on his, the lips drawn back into a thin, sneering smile. The three barkeeps were standing quite still, faces frightened, eyes watching him cautiously, guessing what was coming and not wanting to be in the middle of any gunplay that might be going. All of the men at the bar, and others spread out around the room, wore shooting irons. Bart noticed all of this in a single, sweeping glance. Very slowly, he turned his head, ignoring Ordway for the moment, knowing that the other would not make his move until he was good and ready. There were two more of Saunders' hired killers at the far end of the bar, eyeing him speculatively. The rest seemed to be the usual crowd with the frockcoated gamblers seated at the five tables in the corner.

At the piano, the short, bald-headed man seated there

still had his hands poised over the keys. A cigarette was balanced precariously on his lower lip and his eyes were staring.

'Keep playing,' said Bart slowly. 'I'm sure you wouldn't want to disappoint Ordway.'

The pianist turned his head slowly, looked towards Ordway and raised his brows interrogatively The gunslammer nodded his head almost imperceptibly. His eyes never left Bart's reflection in the large mirror at the back of the bar. The tinny melody started up again, but it was clear that the pianist's heart and soul weren't in his playing.

Very slowly, Bart edged his way forward. Jess Ordway stiffened abruptly at the sudden movement and his fingers were clawed slightly on the top of the table, eyes slitted.

'Hear you were looking for me, Ordway,' said Bart quietly. 'I guess you've found me.'

'You sure seem mighty anxious to die, cowpoke,' said Ordway thinly. He shifted in his seat, then got smoothly, cat-like to his feet. His eyes flicked over Bart appraisingly. 'I hear from Jeb Saunders that you killed a friend of mine – Ed Wiley. That wasn't a very sensible thing to do.' There was a smooth purr to his voice, but Bart had the impression that he wasn't quite as sure of himself as he wanted others to believe. Maybe, in the past, the men he had sought had tried to flee the town, rather than face his guns.

'Make your play whenever you feel like it, Ordway,' snapped Bart thinly. He moved further into the room. Out of the corner of his eye, he saw the men lined along the bar moving nervously to one side. But the three men at the far end did not move. They were watching every move he made, eyes alert, hands very close to their irons. He knew that he was outnumbered in this saloon, that Ordway had picked his spot very carefully, taking every precaution. None of those men would hesitate to draw on him the moment he relaxed his vigilance, he knew that as surely as he knew anything.

'Better warn your outriders to keep their hands away from their irons,' he said tautly, 'unless they want to die with you.'

Ordway's mouth widened in a sneer. 'You talk big, Nolan,' he grated, 'but you're just a little man.' There was a strange glint in his eyes and Bart could read the danger in his face. Very soon now, he would make his move.

'Mebbe so. But this is where you hit the end of the trail, Ordway.' There was a hardness in Bart's tone that made the other straighten up sharply. He moved forward a couple of paces and Bart saw that his retort had stung the other as perhaps nothing else could. His body seemed to tense itself, muscles bunching.

'I'm waiting for you to make your play, Ordway. There ain't goin' to be anybody here who says I drew on you first.'

'Why you goddarned fool!' The other spat the words out. For a moment he opened his mouth wide, then snapped it shut with an audible click. The tension and the silence drew out unbearably as he eased himself forward, clear of the table, his hands hovering over the guns in their holsters. Then, swiftly and suddenly, with a snarled oath, he went for his irons. His hands streaked for the guns with the speed of a striking snake, but they were only halfway out of their holsters when Bart fired, first one and then the other.

Jess Ordway stumbled forward as the slugs tore into his chest. There was a look of stark, stupefied amazement on his face before the muscles slackened. His guns flamed once as he pitched forward on to the floor, the bullets chewing into the wood. The table fell over on to its side, pitching the cards across the floor.

He was dead before he hit the ground and as he swung

round instinctively, Bart saw the other three men going for their guns. Whirling savagely, he went down on one knee beside the bar, throwing lead as he did so. He had a swift, unfocused view of two of the men crouching down behind an overturned table which had been felled with a swift blow of one of the men's foot. Their guns were weaving in an arc as they tried to bring them to bear on him.

Acting on instinct, he slitted his eyes against the flash of their weapons, then he fired. The shots made a hard, metallic rattle as they exploded in the room. He was not baffled by the stabbing explosions of the guns or the stench of the powder smoke in his nostrils. He knew almost exactly where the three men were and saw one of them stumble to his knees, pulling the table over on top of him.

A deafening crash from the far corner and the mirror behind the bar splintered into a thousand glittering fragments that jumped from the wall and fell on to the bar. Somebody yelled an oath.

Bart sucked in a deep breath and steadied himself. This was a little more than he had bargained for. He knew that the majority of the ordinary, decent citizens in Nashville would be against what Jeb Saunders and his hired killers were trying to do, but he doubted whether any of them would have the guts to come out on his side now that he was in trouble, even if he was fighting their battles for them. They knew too much about this man, of the terrible stranglehold he had on this territory for them to risk their lives to help him.

Gripping his guns hard, he stared into the smoke which swirled and eddied about him, feeling the crush of the men around him, and the hurried thumping of his own heart which kept in uneven step with the breathing of the two surviving killers who seemed to be intent now on stalking him from two different directions, hoping to confuse him and take him from two sides.

He fired instinctively, and knew from the sudden grunt that his bullet had hit home. A dark, vaguely-seen shadow moved swiftly behind the tables as he brought up his guns and fired again.

'This is where you get it, Nolan,' hissed a hard voice. Whirling, Bart tried to pinpoint the man's position, but with the smoke haze it was impossible to be sure. His skin was beginning to crawl and he felt the sweat gathering in little pools on his body. But now he was suddenly done with fear, done with the waiting. He fired in the direction of the voice and the answering blast of fire was immediate and accurate.

The gun flame was an orange plume in the dimness among the tables. The bullet thunked into the side of the bar behind him, splintering the wood in a deep gash. Bart fired a second shot, swift and sure, knowing now where the other was. He heard the killer fall, stumbling heavily forward.

Two dead, and one more to go, he thought grimly. The odds were shortening rapidly. He fired again, the muzzle of the Colt tulipping flame. Glass tinkled as more fire came for him from the far corner of the saloon. Bart drew in deep breaths of air that were tainted by the acrid stench of gunsmoke. He wriggled forward keeping his head low, reaching out with his right hand. His fingers touched something soft and yielding. It was Ordway's body. The man's features were still frozen into that mask of stunned surprise, even in death and he still held his gun in his right hand.

Thwuck!!! The bullet hit the top of the table close to his head and ricocheted off into the distance with the whine of tortured metal. Bart crashed down to the floor and pressed himself hard into the body of the man who had tried to kill him. A second slug ploughed into the wooden floor scant inches from his head.

When he started to move again, he edged forward with his shoulders hunched, knees bent slightly and he held his Colts tightly in the palms of his hands, hammers at full cock. He grinned once when he remembered that look on Ordway's face, the look of a man who had died in the instant that he had realized that someone had finally beaten him to the draw. But the grim amusement was shortlived as a gun blasted flame less than three yards away. The man was still crouched near the corner, hidden behind the tables and chairs. Bart heard the faint slithering sound as he shifted his position slightly. The movement sounded as if he had softly shifted his weight from one foot to the other. Bart moved again, stealthily, drifting forward inch by inch, scarcely daring to breathe. It came to him then that the other was probably busy reloading. Raising his guns, he lunged forward, then threw himself swiftly sideways and fired in the same moment.

'I'm right here, killer,' he snarled. Rolling over as he spoke, he fired again, but the other was too quick for him. The shot missed by several inches and he threw another at the man. There was a sudden movement and sound as someone slipped through the bat-wing doors and Bart jerked his head around instinctively. The other must have sensed that he was slightly off guard at that instant, for he rose savagely to his full height, guns studding the dimness with lances of flame. Something seemed to burn its way along Bart's right shoulder, and he almost released his hold on his gun. Then the other was running swiftly for the doors. Sighting swift and sure, Bart let the hammers off his thumbs. The two bullets caught the killer in the middle of the back as he clawed his way forward, hands pawing futilely at the air in front of his stricken face.

The gun-slick hit the floor just inside the doors and lay still.

Carefully, Bart pushed himself up to his full height,

threw a swift glance around the room, then walked forward, prodding the man with the toe of his boot. He saw the mess of blood on the killer's back and knew that he was dead. Pushing open the doors, he stepped outside into the street. He felt suddenly tired of death and the smell of gunsmoke cloying at his nostrils. Jess Ordway was dead and three of his followers. He didn't doubt at all that Jeb Saunders would be forced to show his hand now.

He holstered his Colts and was standing there, sucking air down into his lungs, when the sound of boots on the sidewalk made him jerk his irons clear of leather once more.

'O.K. Hold it, Nolan, we've got rifles trained on you from the other side of the street.'

Bart relaxed. Out of the corner of his eye, he saw the men crouched down behind the rain barrels on the far boardwalk and knew that what the other had said was no idle threat. He holstered his gun. The man who came forward wore a star on his shirt. His gun covered Bart as he walked softly forward. Reaching out, he removed the guns from Bart's holsters and let them drop on to the dirt.

'Reckon you'd better come with me, stranger,' he said in a hard voice. 'You can make yourself at home in jail.'

Bart let his hands hang loosely by his sides. A reckless grin played around the corners of his mouth. Maybe Saunders had begun to play his hand already.

'You one of Foley's deputies?' he asked quietly.

'That's right.' The other smiled coldly.

'Then what's the charges?'

'Disturbing the peace, assaulting the law officer in town and murder.'

Bart's wide mouth set in a determined line. This was a frame if he had ever seen one. He could guess what kind of justice he would get in this town, but that had been a risk he had been forced to take. It still hadn't forced Jeb

Saunders out of his hole; he was letting his hirelings do the dirty work for him. But with those rifles trained on him from the other side of the street, it would be both futile and senseless to try to make a break for it. The other deputies came over, their rifles trained steadily on him in the harsh sunlight. He recognized two of them as men from the Saunders ranch. But there was no recognition in their eyes and their faces were hard and set. Saunders had certainly wasted no time, Bart thought grudgingly.

'Git along to the jailhouse,' said the deputy thinly. 'I guess you already know the way. Sheriff Foley is waitin' for you there.'

Inside the jailhouse, the sheriff was seated in the chair behind the desk. Bart felt a thrill of satisfaction as he saw the man's puffed face and closed right eye. There was a smear of dried blood on his cheek and his arm was in a rough sling. His face twisted murderously as Bart was brought in. He got slowly to his feet and lurched forward until he stood in front of Nolan.

'Wal, reckon we aren't quite so sure of ourselves now, are we?' he gritted. His right hand lashed back, then struck hard at Bart's jaw. He went staggering back on his heels, almost fell, but two of the men held him up, ready for the next blow. Foley rained blow after blow on him until he was satisfied. Then he went back to his desk.

'Throw him inside,' he snarled viciously. 'I haven't finished with him yet. He'll regret what he did this afternoon before he dies. By the time I'm through with him, he'll be begging for death.'

'Think we ought to let Saunders know, Sheriff?' muttered one of the deputies doubtfully. 'He said we were to tell him when we had Nolan.'

'I give the orders as far as this office is concerned,' snapped the other. 'There's plenty of time to tell Saunders. He won't get outa this jail and we have him on

71

a murder charge now. I figure it oughtn't to be too difficult to get the townsfolk worked up enough for a
lynchin'.'

'Maybe we ought to tell Saunders first,' protested one
of the other men, the tall man who had brought Bart in.
'He mightn't like it if we were to hang him before he saw
him.'

'Goddamn you, these are his orders. He wants this man,
Nolan, dead – and he doesn't care how it happens. That
fool Ordway was to be the one to do it but he slipped up.
Now it's up to us.'

Bart licked his lips as the other hustled him towards the
cell door. 'Reckon you people have some funny kind of
laws in this town,' he said thinly, through bruised lips.
'When you can hang a man without givin' him a fair trial.
I suppose you figure you can keep this affair quiet when
the County judge comes around.'

'We'll manage, Nolan,' snapped Foley. His pale eyes
stabbed into Bart's as he lowered himself painfully into the
chair. 'Reckon you'll find that out soon enough.'

Inside the cell, as the door clanged shut, Bart sank
down on the low bed against one wall. His whole body
ached and there was the smooth slickness of blood on his
shoulder where the killer's bullet had ploughed into the
flesh. Gently, he eased the sodden shirt away from the
skin, gritting his teeth as it pulled on the wound. There
was no water to wash with and he knew that Foley was in a
savage mood, and would deny him some, even if he asked.
He lay back on the low, hard bunk and surrendered
himself to the fatigue which dragged at his muscles.

Through the bars of the cell, he could just see Foley,
still seated at the desk and knew that the sheriff was not
going to let him out of his sight until he had exacted retri-
bution for the hiding he had received. Deep down inside,
he wondered what kind of death Foley had planned for

him. It would most likely be something spectacular. He would want every citizen in town to know how he had humbled this man who had broken his wrist. Foley was the kind of man who would never forget a thing like that, decided Bart.

Outside, through the barred window of the cell, he could hear the ordinary, everyday sounds of the town. The street was coming to life now that the sun was westering, bringing a little coolness to the air; and the excitement of the gunfight in the saloon had died down. Some of those people out there, in particular the homesteaders, would be decent folk from way back east, seeking only a new land in which they could start their lives anew after the violence and heartbreak of the war just past. All they wanted was a country where they could grow up without fear, where they could raise their children, sink their roots in peace and away from all bitterness.

But they would never find a life such as that in this country until men such as Jeb Saunders and the vicious circle of killers that he had gathered about him, were destroyed. That was what he, as a deputy marshal, had been assigned to do. Only it seemed he had walked right into a hornet's nest. Certainly he was in the toughest spot of his entire career. These men had him at their mercy and they were determined that he should die, rather than find out any more about them, or tell what he already knew.

'You still figgering on hanging me without a trial, Foley?' he called, without lifting himself from the bunk.

'That's the general idea, Nolan. We don't allow killers like you to go on living when we have the means of stopping you, right here. Besides, the circuit judge won't be in Nashville for another three months. We don't aim to waste good money and food keepin' you here when the verdict will be the same.'

73

'When do you figger on hanging me?'

The other scraped back his chair, got heavily to his feet and walked ponderously towards the door of the cell. Reaching it, he gripped the bars tightly with the fingers of his good hand so that the knuckles stood out whitely under the skin with the nervous pressure he was exerting. 'See no reason why you shouldn't know Nolan,' he grated. 'We're hanging you tonight – at sundown. Mebbe Saunders will be here to see you dangling at the end of a rope, mebbe not. That's up to him, I guess. But he'll be told as soon as you're dead, even if he doesn't come in person.'

Bart shook his head slowly. 'He won't be here if I know Saunders,' he said tightly. 'He wouldn't run the risk of having his name connected with anythin' like this, just in case things might turn out different in the future. He'll leave men like you to take the blame for murder. Then you won't be able to wriggle outa it, although he'll be in the clear.'

'If you're figgering that you can turn us against him with lies like that, you're plumb loco.' The other glared at him through the bars. 'Besides. it'll give me the greatest pleasure I've ever had to see you dangling at the end of that rope.'

'Could be that you'll find yourself there some day if you go through with this,' Bart forced evenness into his voice. 'The people of this town aren't going to stand for murder and corruption much longer you know. One day they're going to take matters into their own hands, and then men like Jeb Saunders will be finished. You can't kill every man in this town, you know.'

'We don't have to.' There was a vicious smile curling the other man's lips as he stood there, grinning down at Nolan. 'Joel Benson was the only man with the guts to stand up to Saunders. You see what happened to him

74

because he was such a goddarned fool. He had the chance to sell out, at a good price too. But he was stubborn as a mule and that cost him his fool life. I liked Benson, in a way. But he ought to have known when to quit.'

'And his daughter. What about her? Think she's made of the same kinda stuff as her father? Figger that she's going to be scared by Saunders and made to sell out for a fraction of the price of that ranch?'

'She'll sell, if she knows what's good for her,' muttered the sheriff viciously. There was something in his tone that sent a little shiver through Bart's body and boded ill for Reva Benson. He had the inescapable feeling that pretty soon, all of the chips would be down, that this entire valley and town was ready to bust wide open in an all-embracing range war.

'Just what do you figger you'll get out of it at the end?'

The other quirked his brows. 'I'm doin' all right for myself with this job,' he grunted. 'And there's security in it, so long as we get ourselves rid of hotheads like you who're likely to start stirring up trouble where none exists.'

Bart lay back, unsettled inside. Slowly, the shadow on the wall began to creep around the side of the cell. The sun was lowering itself towards the western hills. Soon, it would be sundown. Once in a while, he could hear sharp cries in the distance and occasionally, too, his keen ears picked out the growing mutter of people, of voices, swelling in anger. He could guess what was happening out there.

Saunders and the sheriff would have sent their agitators out to work up the people. What lies they would tell, would be of little consequence, so long as the mass of the townsfolk believed them, even for one night. After they had strung him up from a convenient tree, some of them might pause and wonder why Sheriff Foley had been so keen to hang him that night, without giving him a trial, but by that time, it would be too late, and they would have driven another nail into their own coffin. In time, of course, the Marshal's Office might send another man down to investigate his disappearance, but from what he had seen of Jeb Saunders, the range-boss was too thorough and careful a man to leave any loose threads lying around anywhere for an investigator to pick up.

'Not be long now, Nolan.' Foley came back and stood at the door of the cell. The vicious grin was back on his thin lips and there was an unholy light in his narrowed, deep-set eyes. Then his voice took on a silky, almost bantering tone. 'Still, we mustn't forget our manners, even at a time like this. You want me to send out for somethin' to eat for you? Won't take long and there ain't no sense in going to the rope on an empty stomach.'

He laughed harshly, even though the effort clearly hurt the bruised muscles of his face and he put up his hand and rubbed his jaw tenderly, his eyes darkening momentarily at the recollection.

Bart swung his legs over the side of the cot and sat up. He nodded. 'Fair enough,' he said quietly. 'A couple of eggs, ham and coffee.'

For a long moment, Foley glanced at him in surprise, then pulled himself together sharply, on balance once more. He walked back into the office and a little while later, Bart heard him calling for one of the deputies. Ten minutes later, the meal arrived. Bart eyed it for a moment, then shrugged his shoulders and fell to, aware that the sheriff's eyes were on him, watching his every move. There were those two important items still inside his riding boot, he reflected, identifying him; he doubted whether they could get him out of this spot. There was even the possibility that if they even suspected who he was, they might try torture to get out of him how much he knew, and how much, if anything, he had been able to get out of this place. No, better that they shouldn't discover that, he decided. If they didn't know who he was, his successor on this case might stand a better chance.

When he had finished eating, the deputy came into the cell and took the plate away. After that, Bart was left alone to his thoughts while outside, he could hear the crowd getting themselves even more worked up against him. The sun was nearly gone now, he guessed. Less than an hour before it was really dark. He got to his feet and began to pace the cell in anxiety. It wasn't exactly that he was afraid to die. He had seen too many good men die in far worse circumstances than this. But it was the thought that he was leaving so much undone, so much evil behind that he might have prevented, if only he had gone about this in a different way, which worried him. If only he had succeeded in getting some message out of the town, back to the Marshal's Office, warned them in some way of what was happening here in Nashville, of what he had found. But he hadn't dare risk the telegraph office with the operator so obviously in the pay of these crooks.

The door of the outer office opened. There was the sound of footsteps and then Foley came in. There was someone behind him and Bart glanced at the man in surprise. Jeb Saunders! He was the last person he had expected to see in town on that particular night; in fact he would have staked anything that the other would have been mighty anxious to stay away.

'Seems that you couldn't take my friendly advice, Nolan,' said Saunders smoothly. He stood outside the cell and looked in at him with a faint smile twitching the corners of his mouth. 'I hear that you've got yourself into trouble. Murder, so the sheriff tells me. That's too bad. They have their own way of dealing with killers in Nashville as you'll soon find out for yourself.'

'I already know what kind of range justice they have here,' said Bart coldly. He felt the tightness growing in him and hoped that it did not show outwardly. 'Your men have been getting through to the townsfolk all afternoon.'

'They've also been very busy erecting a brand new gallows at the edge of town,' said the other. He slipped his hands into the pockets of his delicately-braided coat. 'It's really a pity that it should have to end like this. I figured you for a much smarter man than you are. Just what is your beef with me, Nolan? Somethin' on your mind – or are you one of these men who try to reform the country? If you are, I figure you must have known it would end in this way.'

'Saunders. You know damned well that I hate your guts,' Bart spat the words out. 'You and your kind will soon be swept from what little power you have. Then there'll be a time of reckoning.'

'Somehow, I don't think so.' The other was unperturbed. He stood quite still, his eyes never moving from Bart's face. 'And even if you are right, you for one, won't be around to see it.'

'Mebbe not. But there'll be others like me who'll come in my place. You can't set yourself up as God and get away with it for ever.'

'I can try. I think you must admit yourself that I'm not doing such a bad job of it at the moment.'

Bart stopped his uneasy pacing and seated himself on the edge of the cot. 'Just why are you here, Saunders?' he demanded. 'Come to make sure that they do a proper job of it this time, and don't bungle it as Wiley and Ordway did.'

'I never leave anything to chance, Nolan. That's one of the big reasons why I'm here now and you're going to die very soon. You take too many risks, you know. That's been your trouble all the time.'

'Guess you'd better be careful not to show yourself. You

don't want the people to know that you're mixed up in it.'

'I'll keep at a discreet distance, I assure you.' The other turned to the sheriff. 'I'm leaving him in your custody, Foley. If anything should go wrong this time—' The threat in his voice was neither veiled nor guarded.

The sheriff blanched and nodded his head quickly. 'We hang him at sundown,' he said tightly. 'Once we've made an example of him, I figger it ought to stop any further outbreaks.'

'Good.' Saunders turned his head and gave Bart a mocking smile as he walked away. 'So long, Nolan. As I said earlier, it's a great pity things had to turn out this way. You're handy with a gun. You could have made quite a name for yourself if you hadn't been so much of a double-crosser.' He went out and a moment later, there was the sound of the outer door being closed.

Foley parted his thick lips, revealing yellowed, stained teeth. 'Another fifteen minutes or so, Nolan,' he said callously. 'Then we string you up.' Turning on his heel, he went back to his desk. Bart sat quite still on the edge of the cot. He could feel the bitterness washing in waves through his mind, into his mouth so that he could almost taste it. Was this what it all came to? Death at the end of a rope. Death at sundown with a crowd of townsfolk looking on, only knowing half of what was really happening in their own town. People who were being roped and branded like steers whether they knew or cared. Here, he thought dismally, were distorted men whose viciousness, avarice and cruelty would have brought about their expulsion from any part of the civilised country.

Fifteen minutes later, they came for him. Foley led the way, his pale face gleaming in the dimness like the belly of a catfish, sweat beading his forehead although the air was cold now that the sun was behind the distant hills. Behind him were four deputies. Two of them held their guns tightly in their fists, while the other two opened up the cell and dragged him out.

'This is the end of the trail as far as you're concerned, Nolan,' said Foley softly. 'Remember what I said this morning. You were goin' to pay for what you did. You busted my arm.'

'I'd do it again, you two-timin' coyote,' snarled Bart. He reeled as the other struck him across the face again with his clenched fist. Then Foley pulled himself together and smiled evilly. 'Let's get it over with,' he said shortly. 'There's no point in waiting any longer.'

They hustled him along the narrow corridor and out the front door of the office, into the street. Bart looked about him instinctively. In front of the office, the dusty street was empty. But at the far end, where it ran out into open country, the gallows had been erected and it was there that the people were. They stood in a silent crowd and watched intently as he walked between his captors, his feet shuffling in the yellow dust.

Foley, leading the way, looked back at him over his shoulder, and his eyes glittered. 'Quite an impressive turnout,' he said thinly. 'At least you have to admit that we carry out our hangings in style here.'

Bart felt the muscles of his stomach tighten convulsively. He looked about him at the faces of the men and women in the street, but saw nothing in them which gave him hope. They watched dully and woodenly as he was forced up to the hastily-improvised gallows.

'Got anythin' to say?' demanded Foley harshly.

'Nothin'.'

The other deliberated that for a moment, then shrugged. He motioned to the two men on either side of gallows. 'Let's get on with it then,' he said thinly. 'We don't have all night to waste.'

One of the men slipped the rope around Bart's neck.

The second watched him warily. If he was to make any move at all, now was when they expected him to make it. But there was nothing he could do. Even if he did manage to get away from these men and their guns, he could never lose himself, even in that crowd. He sensed that although they might not wholly agree with what was happening, they would never come out into the open against Jeb Saunders and help him to escape.

He felt the rope jerk against his throat. The roughness of it chafed his skin and for a moment, he struggled instinctively against it. Out of the corner of his eye, he saw the broad grin on Foley's face. He was nursing his busted arm by his side but for the moment, he was oblivious of any pain there might be in the limb. This was what he had waited for all of that day, He nodded to the two men and stepped back a little way. Bart tensed himself desperately for the savage jerk which would hurl him into eternity. There was a dull roaring in his ears, a sound which he couldn't identify.

Then, over everything, over the muted shouting of the crowd, over the thumping of his own heart against his ribs, there came the sharp and unmistakable bark of a Winchester. The next instant, the pressure around his throat slackened. He could breathe again, could force air down into his aching lungs and see again, although vision swam behind tears which threatened to blind him for a moment.

'Don't any of you rattlers make a move for your guns, or I'll blast you where you stand,' There was a note of menace in that voice, and gradually, Bart realized that it was familiar, that he had heard it some place before. It came again, harsh and insistent. 'Think you can get down from there, Mister?'

Bart shook his head to clear it, then screwed up his eyes, peering into the dimness. He realized now what that drumming noise had been.

A buckboard had driven up and was now standing in

the middle of the street. Seated in it were Reva Benson, a rifle in her hands, and her foreman. There were half a dozen other men astride Palominos ranged along the sides of the street, their sixes drawn. They looked dangerous and determined men.

'Come on down, Mister Nolan,' said the girl urgently. 'We don't have long to waste here.'

'You ain't goin' to get away with this,' snarled Foley savagely. He took a step forward, then halted as if he had been struck as Jed's gun came up to cover him. 'I suppose you know that you're tryin' to interfere with the course of justice,' he blustered.

'Justice!' snapped the girl. 'Jeb Saunders' kind of justice! We all know what that means.'

'A quick hanging without any trial,' said Jed harshly as Bart clambered down into the street, flexing his hands and legs. Reaction would set in soon. It was inevitable after what he had just been through, and he wanted to be well away before that happened. Besides, Saunders would be watching from some vantage point and he wouldn't let him slip through his fingers again without making some kind of a fight for it.

He reached the buckboard and swung himself up beside the girl as Jed scrambled down, his rifle covering the others. 'Now get this buggy outa town and back to the ranch, Miss Benson,' Jed said hoarsely. 'Me and the boys will hold 'em off for a little while, give you enough time to get away.'

'And then what do you figger on doing?' sneered Foley. 'We'll have a posse out after you before dawn. And if you reckon you can hold out in that shack of yourn against the men I can swear out, you're all bigger fools than I take you for.' He was still blustering, but he suddenly changed his tone as he addressed the girl. 'Now see here, Miss Benson. I know how you must feel about your father, but that man you've just allowed to escape this rope is the one who shot him in the back. We have plenty of proof of that. It was for the murder of your father that we were goin' to hang him right now. If you let him go, you'll regret it as long as you live. How do you know he won't kill you and take the place over for himself?'

'The same way that I know he didn't kill my father,' declared the girl quietly. There was a calm firmness in her voice which startled even Bart.

Handing her rifle to Bart, she pulled on the reins, turning the horses. Over her shoulder, she said: 'You sure you can handle them, Jed? I don't want any more blood-letting if I can help it. But if you come for me, Sheriff, you'd better bring your posse with you, because I'll shoot any man who sets foot on my spread.'

'Believe me, you're making a big mistake,' said Foley tightly. For a moment, Brad thought he would go for his gun, using his good arm to attempt to shoot it out with them. But the ring of guns around them stopped him and he forced himself to relax, the iron still in its holster.

Reva Benson flicked the whip over the horses and moments later, they were galloping out of town, along the dusty trail which led to the west. It was dark now, but they still had to pass the Saunders spread on the way and Bart had the feeling that somehow, Jeb had foreseen that this might happen, and had prepared for it. If he had, it meant they might have a fight on their hands before they reached the comparative safety of the Benson ranch.

'You're risking a lot doing this for me,' he said, turning to the girl.

She flashed him a smile. 'You're the only man who can help us now,' she said simply. 'If only those fools back in town would realize it too, we might stand a chance. As it is at the moment, the cards are stacked against us all along the line.'

FIVE

THE WAITING GUNS

While his every nerve screamed action at him, urging him to stay and fight, not to let Jed and the others remain back there to hold off Foley and his men, caution told him that this was the only way out for the time being. Those men knew this country like the backs of their hands. If anyone could give Foley and his posse the slip in this wild country which skirted the Saunders range, they could. Besides, said a little voice in his mind, one man couldn't make a decisive difference.

They hit the trail leading out of town at a fast gallop and held it, the buckboard swaying dangerously as the girl guided the team of horses around the sharply angled bends in the trail. Her features seemed set into a mask of grim determination now. Bart could guess why. They still had several miles to go and if Saunders was able to alert his men, they would hit the trail, if not in front of them, not far behind them and there would be more of them than fleas on a mangy cur.

He settled himself straight in the buckboard, throwing

swift glances into the darkness behind him. The horses leapt forward into a fast lope that threatened to hurl them off the buggy at any moment. Bart did not urge the girl to slow their speed. He did not know how close to the Lazy V ranch they were and he wanted to be safely clear of it. The dark trees wheeled past them on both sides and Bart felt as if he were in the centre of a maelstrom of whirling horses as the girl slashed at them with the whip. He had a brief and confused impression of hoofs striking rock as the animals bounded forward and felt certain that the buckboard must surely leave the trail and hurl them both out into the scrub.

They skirted the Saunders' spread well to the north, keeping the tall pines between the Lazy V and themselves. In the distance, the Lazy V wire glimmered faintly in the yellow moonlight, but as yet there was no sign of any pursuit.

'Think you can hold those horses, Miss Benson?' he yelled as the buckboard swayed precariously. The rearing creatures were like wild things now, having felt the slashing sting of the whip, thundering hoofs striking the ground.

'I can manage.' Her voice was a shout to be heard above the thunder of the horses' hoofs, but clear and firm, without any trace of fear in it. 'Can you see anyone behind us?'

He twisted in his seat, peered into the moonlight which lay at the back of them. The trail, as far as he was able to see, was empty. Then he glanced in the direction of the trees a quarter of a mile distant, where they bounded the coarse scrubland, and smiled grimly to himself. If Sutton were leading the Lazy V hands, as seemed likely, he would not take the direct trail to follow them, but would play it crafty and cunning, preferring to ride parallel with their trail for a while, until he felt sure of himself, and could strike wherever and whenever he chose. He, too, had a score to settle with Bart, but he would go warily now, remembering what had happened to the other killers who had tried to slay him. Any man who could outdraw Ed Wiley and Jess Ordway would be dangerous, even if armed only with a rifle.

It was dark among the trees, impossible for Bart to make any pattern out of the shadows and a horse, he knew, would make little sound, if any, on that carpet of pine needles which lay thick along that dimly-lit trail. When they came into the wide swale that led in a slight twist to the higher end of the valley, further to the west, Bart began to feel that perhaps they might succeed in getting back to the Benson spread without any trouble. He doubted whether any of the sheriff's men could reach them from town and so far, the men of the Lazy V had made no move. He thought ahead through the steps of the make-shift plan which had been forming in his mind ever since he had escaped the noose.

Someone had to get out of the valley and give warning to the U.S. Marshal's Office of what was happening here. He would have gone himself, but that would mean leaving this girl to the tender mercies of Jeb Saunders and the sheriff. After what she had done tonight, they would be determined to kill her and her men as they had murdered her father. Jeb Saunders would be almost beside himself with fury right now, he thought grimly, now that he knew that Bart had somehow succeeded in slipping through his fingers once more. No, he would have to remain here, on the Circle W, face whatever might come, and try to send someone else out.

A sudden, sharp movement among the trees to their left brought him up with a jolt. He twisted round on the buckboard to get a better look, although he knew instinctively what it had been, There was a closely-packed bunch of them, cutting down out of the trees. It was clear that he had been right on their moves. He couldn't recognize any of them at that distance but they came charging down the side of the swale, shrieking like the bunch of coyotes they were.

Bart gritted his teeth. 'Here they come!' he shouted warningly. 'I'll try to hold them off with the rifle. How much further to the spread?'

'Another couple miles or so.'

He felt a stab of despair. Those men out there would have fresh horses. They could overhaul them long before they reached the Circle W wire. Swinging the rifle, Bart fired, but his shot went wild. His mouth set grimly as he twisted on the buckboard. In front of them, he knew, the trail ran fairly straight and level for several miles. But in spite of this, the vehicle was bumping and swaying savagely from side to side, making it almost impossible to steady the rifle for a killing shot. The riders of the Lazy V swept nearer and he could see the brief stabbing of the gunflames from their Colts.

'Keep low,' he shouted to the girl. The bullets were falling short but the range was closing rapidly as the riders swung down to hit the trail a little distance behind them, then swung their horses to follow them. The leading man fired again and the slug bit through the air close to Bart's shoulder. In the moonlight, he realized grimly, they made a perfect target. He sent two more shots blasting back, saw one of the riders stumble, then pitching from his saddle, he hit the dirt, rolled over and lay still. The riderless mount thundered on.

The girl did not slow their speed; and Bart could not know how near they were to the Circle W wire but he knew that they had to be well clear of that before these men would give up their determined pursuit. The girl would probably have left the rest of her men on the ranch, ready for just such an emergency as this; although she probably hadn't figured on Saunders having time in which to warn his men on the ranch. Somebody must have lit out of town at high speed, he mused tightly.

They hit the level ground of the swale with the riders close behind and closing ground rapidly. More slugs sang over their heads as they crouched low over the buckboard. He threw a swift glance at the girl, saw the white blur of her face close to his, illuminated by the moonlight. Her lips were set tight across the middle of her features, but though her eyes were bright, there was no fear in them. Savagely, filled with a consuming anger, he sent two more shots into the milling pack on their heels. A horse reared, then swerved suddenly and his foot and leg went deep into a gopher hole at the side of the trail. The mount squealed and went sliding down, forelegs sprawling. The rider was thrown clear over the animal's neck and hit the ground in a rolling spin. He hadn't been killed by the fall, Bart saw, but he would be out of the pursuit and that was one less killer he had to deal with.

He twisted his head back to the front. Ahead of them, the trail wound straight and true, into the narrow valley which he knew led directly to the Circle W range. They were still not out of trouble. The nearest rider was less than two hundred yards behind. The stabbing flashes of orange flame from his sixes cut through the night. Slugs ploughed into the wood close to Bart's shoulder. The minutes dragged. The moon slid behind a cloud and darkness spread quickly over them. For a moment, the others held their fire. They couldn't see them clearly, thought Bart, but the killers had one big advantage. They knew that the buckboard had to stay on the trail, whereas they could sweep around in both directions and take them from the sides.

Gun thunder echoed in the narrow valley as they plunged into it. There was a sudden surging forward of

men and horses from all directions. He lifted the rifle
again, squeezed the trigger as a dark shadow flashed by.
The man uttered a shrill yell and rolled out of the saddle,
hitting the ground with a dull thump, rolling over on to
his side. There was now an icy coldness in Bart's brain,
which washed away everything else, every other emotion.
Then they had burst clear of the narrow valley, were in the
open again and suddenly there were other tongues of
flame leaping out of the darkness ahead of them. One of
the killers, almost alongside the buckboard suddenly
threw up his arms and fell back, clawing at his face as he
rolled back out of sight. Seconds later, they were through
the gap in the Circle W fence and the Lazy V riders were
wheeling their horses desperately as they fought to get
away from the murderous fire which met them.

'Give them murderin' polecats lead,' yelled a harsh
voice from the darkness. Instantly, more gun flashes
replied along the edge of the range. The men of the Circle
W had been deployed well. Beyond the wire the men who
had been pursuing them could easily be trapped against
the tall walls of the valley. Bart had a brief glimpse of
Sutton, neck-reining his horse in a desperate attempt to
swing it clear of the intense fire that poured into the
killers. He cursed and roared as the rest of his men
ducked out, urging the gunslammers to stand and fight.

But for the time being, they had had enough of lead.
Chasing a man and a girl across the plain, when they
outnumbered them three or four to one was good sport as
far as they were concerned. But when the tables were
turned on them, when the fight became a little more even,
they wanted nothing of it.

'You all right, Miss Benson?' One of the men came
forward, holstering his sixes.

'Sure. I'm fine, Matt,' she replied as Bart helped her
down from the wagon. 'Seems we just made it.'

'Those *hombres* won't be coming back for a little while,' said the other grimly. 'If they do, we'll be waitin' for 'em.'

'When they do come, they'll have more men with 'em,' said Bart tightly. 'The sheriff will be swearing out every roughneck in the county by now. This is the showdown. Saunders will be coming with the rest of his men before morning. You know what happened to the Thompson spread? They'll fire this and kill every man and woman here.'

'We've got rifles and guns,' declared the girl passionately. 'They murdered my father just because he wouldn't sell out to them. Do you think I'm going to let him down now.'

'That's the spirit,' said Matt brusquely. 'We're behind you all the way, Miss Reva.'

Bart stood indecisive, frowning. 'How long before the rest of your men get back here, Miss Benson?' he asked.

'They ought to be here in another hour. Why? Have you got something in mind?'

'Could be. It's a slim chance, but one we've got to take. You know I'm a U.S. Deputy Marshal. I was sent here to look into the affairs of Jeb Saunders. I still haven't found out everything I'd like to know about him. But the chips are down now. He wants me dead. He wants you dead, too. But if I can get word through to the Marshal's Office in Bluff Creek, we stand a chance.'

'We can hold off these *hombres* if they decide to come again,' said Matt, a thin smile on his grizzled features. 'We've got twenty-seven men who can handle a gun, once Jed and the boys get back here from town. How long you reckon it'll take you to get to Bluff Creek, mister? We can give yuh a fresh horse.'

Bart shook his head. 'I'm not goin',' he said quietly. 'I've got to find out more about Saunders. Now that his hand has been forced, he might panic and make a mistake. At least, that's what I'm hopin' for. There must be somebody in Nashville who knows his secret, or somewhere that I might find it.'

'The only man who could help you on that matter would be Ed Sefton. He's the editor of the Clarion. If anybody knows about Jeb Saunders, he's your man.'

'You figure he might talk to me?'

'Could be. He's straight, but scared at times. Mostly, now, he prints what Jeb Saunders tell him to. But he ain't no friend of that killer's.'

'Let's go up to the ranch,' suggested Reva Benson. 'The boys will stay here and watch for Jed. If Sutton and his men do come back, they'll be waiting for them.'

Bart said nothing, but settled himself down on the buckboard as they drove slowly to the ranch. It was far smaller than Jeb Saunder's place, but comfortable and tastefully furnished. He sank down thankfully into the chair before the fire with a deep sigh.

'I'll get you somethin' to eat,' she said from the doorway. 'You must be plain tuckered out after what happened tonight.'

'If it hadn't been for you, I'd have been dead by now. I reckon I owe you a lot.'

'Just bring my father's killer to justice and I'll have been amply repaid.' There was a quiet hate in her voice and he looked round at her, startled for a moment. Looking at her standing in the doorway, he saw for the first time, the full measure of her fear and grief, and suddenly he passed his hand down his cheek, confused. She must have lived most of her life in such close communion with the hate which had spread itself out over this territory, he thought and it had, inevitably, left its mark on her. But there was a clear spark in her wide, grey eyes which still burned brilliantly in spite of everything she had been through.

'You know it's a pity that the other folk in Nashville

don't think and act the same way as you do,' he said quietly. 'If they did, we'd soon be rid of Saunders and his kind.'

'They're afraid,' she told him quietly. 'They've seen what Saunders did to my father and to the Thompsons.' She went into the kitchen and Bart leaned back in the chair, allowing his whole body to relax. He straightened when he heard the heavy drum of hoofs. A horse slid to a halt before the door of the ranch and boot heels rapped hastily across the porch boards. The door opened and Jed stood framed there for a moment. He looked grim and dangerous.

'Sheriff Foley is swearing in every deputy he can find to form a posse. Reckon they'll be over this way in about an hour or so.'

'Just what I figgered he'd do. This is more of Saunders' work.' Bart got to his feet and paced back and forth. He halted finally, glancing at the big foreman. 'D'you reckon you could make leather to Bluff Creek, Jed? I've got to get word through to the Marshal's Office there. We need help here if we've to defeat Saunders. And we can't fight him ourselves.'

'What yuh figger on doin'?'

'Jeb Saunders knows I'm here. He knows that he's got a fight on his hands, but he's been gettin' ready for this in plenty of time. He's got the biggest bunch of owlhoots and killers this side of the Mississippi. If they do attack us here, we might be able to hold out for a couple of days but unless we get help by then, we're finished. Just get through to the Marshal, tell him my name and everythin' that's happened. He'll know what to do.'

'And what about Miss Benson?' demanded the other harshly.

'Believe me, I'd like to see her out of this. But Saunders may have men watching the trail and one man might stand a chance whereas two could be spotted. She'll be as safe here as the rest of us.'

'You'll need a fresh horse, Jed,' said Reva from the doorway. 'Better get one from the corral and move out as quickly as you can.'

The foreman hesitated. 'I'd feel better if I stayed here and killed a few of those polecats,' he said thinly.

'Sure you would, Jed,' said the girl. She laid a hand on his arm. 'But we need somebody who knows this country, who can push a horse to the limit. You know these parts better than any other man on the ranch. You're the logical man to go.'

'All right, if you reckon I should.' He threw wide his big arms in a gesture of surrender. He went outside and through the window Bart saw the big man walk to the corral and pick out one of the horses. He had it saddled within minutes, then walked it to the ranch and came back inside.

'I'm ready to move out,' he said thickly. 'Just what do you want me to tell this Marshal?'

'Simply that I have to stay here to get more evidence against Jeb Saunders, but that we need help right away. We can't trust the telegraph agent and the sheriff is in Saunders' pay. He'll understand.'

'Saunders is bound to make his play before dawn. You'll need every man you've got if you're to hold him off.'

'We'll make out,' said the girl quietly. There was a note of confidence in her deep voice. 'Don't worry about us, Jed. Just hurry back with the help.'

Bart watched the big foreman ride away into the darkness. He hoped that the other would get through, for all of their sakes. It was the best part of two days' ride into Bluff Creek and another two days coming back. He felt the old bleakness stirring inside him. He doubted if they could hold out against Jeb Saunders for that long. Their only hope lay in the fact that, so long as Saunders did not know anyone had gone for help, he might hold his hand a little in case he overplayed it. There was a streak of vicious cruelty in that man which had manifested itself on several occasions in the past. He was the sort of man who preferred that his victims should suffer, rather than that they should have a quick death. He might decide to play with them for a while. If he took that course, then they might stand a chance.

He went back to the chair, fashioned himself a quirly and drew deep on the tobacco. It helped him with his thinking and now, as never before, it was essential that he should think straight.

Reva Benson came back into the room. She said quietly: 'You look as though you could do with some sleep, Bart.'

He shook his head. 'Those killers will be back soon.'

'All the more reason why you should get some rest. The boys are watching the trail in from town. They'll give us plenty of warning before Foley and his gang arrive.'

'Mebbe you're right,' Reaction had set in and his brain was humming with it. He checked the twin Colts which Jed had provided for him, slid them into the holsters and settled himself down in the chair. He needed sleep, he told himself; he could feel the toll of the strain of that day, of the closeness to death, and of that long ride back through the moonlight and darkness to the Circle W ranch. When Foley and his men came, he would be ready for them.

He slept fitfully and when he roused, it was almost dawn. He sat upright, not taking his time at coming to full awareness, as he usually did. He went into the other room, but the girl was not in it, and the whole house was silent. For a moment a feeling of panic swept over him. Had Foley been while he had slept? He dismissed the thought instantly. That was impossible. He was a light sleeper and would have woken instantly at the first sign of trouble.

94

Then the outer door opened and the girl came in. She smiled up at him, but there were faint lines of strain on her face.

'Anythin' happened?' he asked quickly.

She shook her head. 'They seem to have drawn off for the time being. Perhaps Jeb Saunders has had second thoughts about trying to attack us.'

'Don't build up any hopes on that,' said Bart grimly. 'He may have some reason for holding out like this, but I can't see it. He's like a rattler coiled to strike. When he does, it'll be quick and sudden, hoping to take us by surprise. Where are the rest of the men now?'

'Out on the range, all but five of them who're around the ranch. I didn't want to take any chances of those killers working their way around from the north and cutting in behind the rest of my men. That's why I kept five here.'

Bart nodded. That had been a wise move on her part. He went outside, took a quick look around the buildings. They seemed to have been solidly built, even the large barn set a little way apart from the ranch itself. They could be easily defended and there was plenty of open space around them all, over which the killers would have to come to get to grips with them. He nodded to himself, satisfied, aware that the girl was watching him from the doorway. A breeze flowed downhill off the range, stirring his neckerchief.

He went back to the girl. 'Think I'll take a ride over and see how the other boys are gettin' on,' he said quietly. 'It might be a mistake if they got caught out there in open rangeland. Jeb's men could cut them to pieces if they rode them down.'

He saw the worried expression that flitted over her regular features. She nodded quickly. 'I've told them that they're to take all their orders from you until this is all over,' she went on slowly. 'I haven't had much dealing with men like Saunders and Foley. I know they're killers and that they probably murdered my father.'

Bart nodded, picked a horse out of the corral and threw a saddle over it. For a few minutes, he sat the saddle then, listening to the silence of the dawn that somehow seemed not quite a silence, having in it many tiny sounds which he couldn't identify, the lingering, lost echoes that might come of men travelling hard in the distance, he wheeled the horse and galloped off towards the east. He put all of his speculation on wondering why Saunders hadn't made his play during the night and found this baffling. Surely, the other must have known that the very first thing he would do, once he arrived at the Circle W, would be to alert all of the men and make the defences ready for an attack. Every minute that Saunders lingered would make it more difficult for him when he finally did decide to attack.

He thought too, as he rode, of Sheriff Foley. Just what kind of kinship was there between these two men? He couldn't see the portly, loud-mouthed sheriff risking his neck in coming out here to make everything look legal; but if Jeb Saunders insisted, then there might be little enough that Foley could do to back down. He could plead that with a broken arm, he would be of no use when it came to gunplay, but there seemed to be some kind of twisted justice inside Saunders that would make him want to make everything appear legal and above-board in the eyes of the townsfolk. His curiosity was constant now and from it came a new purpose. His plan had been to wait until Saunders and his men attacked, backed no doubt by the posse which Foley had been quick on forming in Nashville, test the strength of the opposition against him, and then figure things out from there. But the fact that, for some reason he couldn't fathom, Saunders had refused to be drawn gave him pause. Now he was more concerned with knowing why Saunders had stayed his hand, than with taking a passive line of resistance for the next four days, hoping to hold out until Jed got back with help.

There was danger in this; there might be a plan being built up against him at this very moment, but he had the feeling that somewhere in Nashville, lay the answers to a lot of the questions concerning Jeb Saunders that were worrying him at that moment. Then he took to thinking about the sodbusters, on the far outskirts of the town. He wondered whether they had realized their danger yet and what they would do if it came to a showdown. They might fight, but one could never be sure. They were the pioneers of this country now and he had the feeling that if it came to the showdown, they would fight to protect their homesteads from men like Saunders. Most of the sodbusters were men who had been through the war, who knew that if you wanted anything you had to fight for it. Now they had their families and their homes to fight for; and not just the abstract ideals for which they had fought in the war.

He entered the timber at the eastern end of the spread, cut in through the trees. He knew roughly where the men would be, watching the trail as it sloped down through the narrow valley. On most other sides, even without the wire, the ground was rough and the pine forests almost impenetrable, even to men on horseback. Soon there was less underbrush and half an hour later, he came out into the open. He found the men resting behind their guns among the rocks which looked down on the trail. They turned at his approach, then relaxed.

'You figger they've given up their idea of attacking us, Marshal Nolan?' asked one of the men as he dismounted and slid down among them.

'They may, but it isn't like Saunders to give up so easy.

He's plannin' somethin', if we only knew what it was. You sure there's no other spot where he might be able to cross the wire?'

'He might try coming down the east face,' said another of the men, 'but he'd be a fool if he tried that. I've known many men who tried it, but none of them ever succeeded. It can't be done.'

Cool wind sifted down from the hill's crest, but the sun was nearly up and pretty soon, Bart decided, it was going to be as hot as the hinges of hell among these rocks. Maybe that was what Foley and the others were waiting for. They listened hard for the hoofbeats which would tell them of the approach of the Lazy V riders, or the posse of roughnecks from town, but heard nothing. After a half hour, when the sun lifted clear of the horizon, there was still silence.

Bart could feel the tension beginning to mount, both in himself and in the others. He could read the hard shine in the men's eyes. They were all weathered men, most of them from Texas way he guessed, some used to the ways of violence, but now filled with grave uncertainties. They had waited through the night for Foley or Saunders to show up. Now they were no longer sure of themselves and Bart could sense that in each man, there was the feeling that they were being led into a trap which they couldn't understand. Bart reached a sudden decision.

'Reckon we'd better hit leather and go back to the ranch,' he said calmly. 'Ain't no point in waitin' out here for them to come to us. Mebbe they're watchin' us right now from those rocks over yonder, waiting for us to make a move. But this ain't an easy place to defend.'

'You figger they'll head in from another direction?' asked one of the men and his voice was strained with excitement.

'I wouldn't like to stake my last dollar that they won't.'

Bart eased himself up into the saddle, waited until the others had done likewise, then turned his sorrel back on to the rutted trail. There was the feel of eyes watching his every move, but he could see nobody and there was only the heat haze beginning to shimmer on the rocks which bounded the trail leading east past the Lazy V spread.

He spurred the horse along the trail, the others galloping after him. The slope to his right and left became a blur, but he had the feeling that this hard riding was necessary now. There was a sense of urgency in him which gave him no rest. At the top of a long rise, he reined his mount and sat quiet, keening the morning air for hoofbeats and the breeze bore to him some ghosts of sounds that were in the distance, dim and at first untranslatable. Then he recognized them for what they were.

Gunshots! He tried to judge the direction from which they came, then whirled on the others and said swiftly, savagely: 'There's trouble at the ranch. Somehow, those owlhoots must have slipped around us, maybe during the night. They could have holed up somewhere until they saw us ride out.'

He put spurs to the horse. It was still fresh enough to want to go and leapt forward so that he let it stretch itself out across the low meadowlands. The others thundered behind him and there was the sound of anger and vengeance in their hoofbeats.

The ravines at the far edge of the meadowland slowed them down, but then they were in the open once more and they could see the ranch in the distance. It looked on the face of things, just as Bart had left it earlier that morning. Then he narrowed his eyes as he saw the faint spurts of flame which came from the windows, heard the sharp barks of the rifles and sixes, and saw the horses which were staked out a little distance away, out of sight from anyone inside the buildings. The killers must have sneaked up on them, leaving their horses tied. But they hadn't been lucky enough. Someone had spotted them coming in and opened fire.

A sudden savage anger bit through Bart as he put his horse to the trail which wound down the slope towards the ranch. His sixes were out, balanced in his palms, and they felt suddenly good. The other men thundered after him.

Nearing the ranch, he reined his mount, slithered from the saddle in one swift, instinctive movement before the horse had stopped, and ran for the cover of the rocks behind the killers. One glance was enough to tell him that this was the posse which the sheriff had sworn in the night before. How they had managed to get there without being seen earlier, was something he couldn't figure. All that mattered now, was that they were there and that the numbers had now been evened. Also, the others had now found themselves in the middle of the fire.

Out of the corner of his eye, he saw the other men with him, sliding from their saddles and running forward, crouching low behind the rocks, their guns out. He saw the fat, portly figure of the sheriff almost directly in front of him, well out of range of the fire from the ranch. The others must have been expecting Sutton and the Lazy V riders to come through and back his play for he still kept his back turned. Thus the sheriff was set for an unpleasant surprise, but he had still kept half of his wariness, for he turned his head after a moment and opened his mouth to yell, raising his good arm in a signal.

Then he stopped. Bart lifted himself slightly so that the other could see who it was. For an instant, Foley squinted up into the glaring sunlight, his mouth opening and closing as he realized how he had fallen into a trap of his own devising. Then he yelled a hoarse order to the men with him. In the same moment, Bart's gun barked savagely and one of the men behind the rocks suddenly threw up his arms and

100

slithered down into an inert heap, almost at Foley's feet.

At once, the posse turned and began firing instinctively. They must have realized that the immediate danger came from behind them now. Bullets sang off the rocks in front of Bart. Another smashing volley rang out from the rocks. The flying lead buzzed around Bart and the others as if they had stirred up a nest of angry hornets, but the men kept up their steady, well-placcd fire. Window glass in the ranch smashed as a bullet cut through it, shattering it into a thousand pieces. But most of the fire, Bart saw, was being directed against them.

'Nolan! Are you there?' Foley's voice rang out above the shots.

Bart turned to the others. 'Hold your fire until I give you the word,' he ordered. 'Let's see what that two-timin' sheriff wants.'

'It's a trap, Marshal,' broke in one of the men savagely. 'He's just playing for time.'

'Mebbe he is, and mebbe he isn't. But I reckon we'd better find out what he wants.'

'What is it, sheriff?' he called. There was a note of deliberate sarcasm in his deep voice, but if the other noticed it, he gave no sign as he yelled back:

'Don't you men know that you're firing at the law? As sheriff round here, I demand that you turn over that murderer Nolan to me. Then we'll pull out. We've got no call to fight the rest of you. He's the man who shot Joel Benson in the back. I can prove that.'

'They ain't listenin' to you, Foley,' shouted Bart. 'Seems to me they know you for what you are.'

'You're all a lot of goddarned fools if you believe him,' was the only answer that Foley made. 'You can't hope to fight the law for ever. If we pull out now without Nolan, we'll be back with more men and you'll pay for this day's work.'

A solitary shot came from the ranch at his words and Bart saw the other throw himself swiftly sideways as the slug whanged off the rock close to his head.

Reva Benson's voice came loud and clear from the house. 'Listen to me, Foley, and hear me good. I know who killed my father and so do the rest of my men. I also know somethin' you ought to know perhaps, somethin' that might have been worrying you.'

'Keep talking, Reva,' Bart yelled. 'Mebbe this will make 'em change their minds.' He knew what was coming next, knew that they would believe it more if it came from her, than from him. He saw no reason now why his identity should remain a secret any longer. If Jed had got through at all, he would be sufficiently far away now and on his way to Bluff Creek, that it was doubtful if any of Foley's men, or Saunders's killers, could catch up with him.

'You've probably been wonderin' why a saddletramp should head into Nashville and then start taking on Jeb Saunders by himself. Mebbe it's time you knew why. Bart Nolan ain't no saddletramp, Sheriff. He's a U.S deputy marshal. You're not the law in these parts any longer.'

Even from where he lay, with his shoulder pressed into the hard rocks, Bart could see the look of consternation on the sheriff's hard features. Then the other shook his head and looked swiftly along the line of men spaced out beside him.

'Lies, all lies!' he shouted. 'This is just a trick, men. He ain't no marshal.'

'That's where you're makin' a big mistake, Foley,' called Bart harshly. 'But we didn't come here to parley with a bunch of crooks like you. Either you git off this range, pronto, or we pump more lead into you.'

On the instant the guns opened up again, Bart searched the rocks ahead of him with keen eyes. There had been a sudden movement there, while he had been talking. He caught it again. Three of the men with Foley were slipping away to their right. He saw instantly what they intended to do. While Foley and the rest of his men kept him occupied, the others were to sneak around to the rear of the ranch, and try to force an entry there. Maybe they figured that if they could get Reva Benson as a hostage, it would swing things completely in their favour.

There was no time to be lost if this manoeuvre was to be stopped. He signalled the men forward with a sweep of his right arm then moved in himself, at a crouching run, head low. There were more shots from the windows, but the three men had slipped away around the rocks and were lost to sight. Swiftly, he ran forward. Now and then a slug came searching for him, but he ran on, streaking for the small clump of trees where he had last seen the three men. He reached it and threw himself down into shadow. They were still less than five yards in front of him, cutting across an open space towards the ranch, their guns glittering in their hands.

SIX

GUNSMOKE

The three of them skirted the fence, keeping low. There was no fire from the windows on that side of the ranch, and Bart couldn't tell if it had been deliberately left unguarded, or if the man watching that side had been killed. He edged forward as the other men climbed the fence and dropped into the yard. His guns moved swiftly and he fired twice. Bullets from the main gang among the rocks skipped around his feet as he darted forward. The cookshack was only a few yards away, but none of the three men were intent on reaching it.

He fired again and in a quick burst of speed, hit the fence and swung himself over it. A slug tore into the wood an inch from his shoulder as he dropped to his knees, rolled over on his side for a couple of feet, then came up, on-balance again, cat-like, guns swinging in his hands. One of the men was lying on his face in the dust of the yard. There was no sign of the others. He paused only long enough to make sure that the gunslammer was dead before running for the wall of the shack. Rounding it, he spotted the two men, close to the ranch, worming their way forward. One of them turned, saw him and fired

104

swiftly, instinctively, Bart had time to recognize the Mexican Kid before the men were around the corner and out of sight again. Now they were at the back of the ranch-house and he knew that it would be a simple matter for them to take the defenders there by surprise, particularly as the others would not be anticipating an attack to the rear. There was still plenty of gunfire at the front of the ranch, directed against the sheriff and his men who were still cornered like rats, among the rocks, caught in the hail of fire from two directions.

Breaking cover, Bart sidled swiftly forward, reached the corner of the ranch-house, gently eased himself around it. For a moment, he glimpsed one of the men on the back porch. There was no sign of the Mexican Kid and he guessed that the killer was already inside the house, leaving the other man on guard.

Bart quickly ran the length of the ranch, taking his life in his hands. The move took the waiting gunman completely by surprise. He had obviously expected to draw fire from the corner of the building and this unexpected move caught him off balance. He tried to bring his sixes to bear on Bart, swinging them up in a blur of movement, fingers squeezing on the triggers in the same instant. The bullets kicked dirt around Bart's feet as he lunged forward. Another slug laid a red-hot brand along his right arm. Then he was on the wooden boards of the rear porch and the man was less than three feet away, eyes staring wildly as he tried to swing round. The cruel lips were twisted back into a fiendish grin. Then Bart's Colts spoke, the guns slamming and bucking against his wrists. The other looked at him for an instant with an expression of stupefied amazement written all over his face. Then the red stain appeared on his shirt and he toppled forward with a tired sigh as his last breath exhaled from his lungs. His guns dropped on to the floor of the porch with a dull clatter a second before his body hit it dully.

The Mexican Kid was somewhere inside, but Bart did not pause. He could be waiting with his sixes aimed on the door, biding his time until Bart stepped inside. Or he could, at that very moment, be running through the house, hoping to take Reva and the others by surprise. Once he had the girl in his hands, it would all be over. They couldn't afford to risk her life, even though with a man like the Mexican Kid, they couldn't take his word even if he gave it.

The short passage at the back of the door was empty. From the front of the house, the roar of sixes still slammed the air. Evidently, the sheriff had decided to fight it out, probably knowing that the Mexican Kid had made it inside, hoping that he could carry out his part in the diabolical plan. Bart gritted his teeth and moved catfooted through the house. Time was running short. Keeping a wary glance on the stairs, he dogged the hammers of his guns back.

Then, a gun blasted from the end of the passage. Swiftly, Bart twisted sideways and threw himself against the wall as the slug hummed through the air where his head had been a moment earlier.

'This is where you get it, Nolan,' said the Kid's silky voice. He was well hidden, close beside the stairs. 'I've been looking forward to this moment for a long time.'

'Seems to me you're doing a mighty lot o' talkin' and nuthin' else,' said Bart scornfully. He was hoping to goad the other into showing himself, even if only for a second.

For a moment, there was no movement, then the Kid showed himself for an instant as he darted across the passage to the other side. Bart snapped an instinctive shot at him, heard the bullet hit the wall and knew that he had missed. The Kid still had the edge on him, could fight where he liked.

'Listen, Kid,' he said tightly, 'I've heard a lot about you, how you're supposed to be one of the fastest gunmen in this territory. I wonder if you're really as fast as they say you are, or whether you're just hidin' behind a reputation you don't deserve.'

Still there was silence, although he imagined he could hear the other man breathing softly in the shadows at the side of the passage.

'If you are trying to taunt me out into the open, *senor*,' said the silky voice at last, 'you are wasting your breath. I came here to get the girl, but if I can kill you at the same time, that will be good. Mister Saunders will like that, I am sure.'

'How're you goin' to kill me? Shoot me in the back like you did Benson?'

There was a sharp intake of breath from the shadows. 'That is a lie, *senor*. I shoot no man in the back. But with you it will be different. I do not take chances with my life. That is why I am still alive today when Wiley and Ordway are dead. I do not know if you are faster than I am, but that is a question which will not be answered, because I shall kill you very soon.'

Bart narrowed his eyes. The gunfire still thundered from the front of the ranch and he figured that Foley was keeping up his attack in spite of having been hit from the rear, simply so that the Kid could go through the house without being troubled. Seconds later, he realized that he had been fooled, that the Kid had been talking in that silky voice of his to lull him into a sense of false security. There had been something oddly hypnotic about that voice and when the Kid moved, it came with the suddenness and the unexpectedness of a striking snake. He threw himself out into the middle of the passage, guns blazing. Bart felt the airlash of a bullet and went down on to his knee against the wooden floorboards, his action instinctive, and it was that which saved his life. Two more slugs hammered into the wall over his head, then the Kid lowered his aim and a bullet struck Bart's gun, sending it spinning from his grasp. His other arm was weak and clumsy where the other slug had creased it and he knew instinctively, that he could never bring the sixer to bear in time. There was just one driving thought in him now. He had come so far and through too much to lose out now. He tried to will his fingers to tighten on the trigger, to lift the gun until it was lined on the other's chest, but it was useless.

He could see the coldly calculating look in the other's grey eyes and thought: This is the finish! Nothing could stop that killer from squeezing the trigger and this time, he would make no mistake. Despair crowded through Bart's mind as he knelt there. The seconds seemed to drag themselves out into individual eternities. The Mexican Kid's knuckles whitened as he took pressure on the trigger.

He braced himself for the smashing impact of the bullet, flinched at the bark of the gun, then suddenly stiffened as he saw the Kid twist slowly where he stood, his features slack, the guns tilted downward from his fingers. He bent at the knees and slumped to the floor of the passage, eyes still wide and fixed as he strove to turn his head and make out the identity of the person who had killed him.

Very slowly, Bart lifted his head and stared at the figure in the doorway, the smoke from the six-gun still curling in the air.

'Is he dead?' asked Reva Benson. There was a little shake to her voice. She took a faltering step forward. Bart got to his feet and led her back into the other room. He nodded as she sank down into one of the chairs. 'He's dead,' he said tightly. 'But you can have something to remember. Apart from Sutton, that was one of the worst enemies of Nashville.'

'Who was he?' she asked, her voice still quavering a little.

'He called himself the Mexican Kid. He was a wanted man like most of the others in Jeb Saunders' pay. Nobody is goin' to miss him.'

'I thought I heard a shot back there and came to take a look. I heard him talking just before I reached the door and guessed what was happening.'

'I'm glad you did. Another couple seconds and he would have killed me,' Bart licked his lips. Pain was jarring redly along his arm where the slug fired by one of the posse had creased it when he had run for the house. He pulled back the sleeve.

'You've been hit,' Reva was on her feet in a moment. 'Better hold still while I clean it up for you. Fortunately, it doesn't look as though it's reached the bone.'

'I'll be all right. What about those polecats outside?' She went over to the window, taking care to keep out of line of fire. There was a note of elation in her voice as she said sharply: 'They're pulling out, Bart. They've had enough!'

He got up and walked over beside her. A volley of shots followed the sheriff and the rest of his men as they fled for their mounts. Two of the posse fell but the others managed to climb into the saddle. Then they were thundering away, throwing lead as they rode off.

Bart nodded slowly. He hadn't expected Foley and the posse to put up much of a fight. It had surprised him that they had fought for so long in the face of the Circle W men. Most of the men in that posse had been recruited from Nashville. They had no real call to fight Reva Benson and her men and had probably only come out with the sheriff because they'd figured that there was little danger to themselves and probably plenty of sport to be had, shooting it out with a girl and a handful of cowpokes. But the cowpokes, and the girl, had fought back as they had never been expected to fight and it was the men from Nashville who were fleeing, leaving their dead behind them.

The ranch hands began moving in, treading warily among the rocks, making sure that all of the men lying there were dead. It was just possible that some of them might be playing possum, waiting to launch another attack when the opportunity presented itself. Reva's bandage was around Bart's arm when he went outside again. One of the men came over to him. He nodded, satisfied.

'Reckon we scared off that bunch o' critturs, Marshal,' he said gruffly. 'They won't be comin' back fer some time after that lickin' they got.'

'We've still got to remember Saunders and his bunch,' said Bart warily. 'They're still around some place. Mebbe they were waitin' to see how Foley would fare. If he'd finished what he set out to do, they could have come in and taken over without loss to themselves but as it is, they'll come pretty soon.'

'Think they'll bring that rat of a sheriff back with 'em?'

'Could be. Saunders must be about at the end of his tether by now. Too many things have gone against him. If he doesn't smash us soon, the people in Nashville, and especially the sodbusters just outside of town might get to figgering that he isn't the big man he claims he is, that he doesn't own this place so long as there are people like us who can fight against him, and beat him. Once that happens, they'll lose their fear of him and start riding against him. When that happens, mark my words, he'll be finished as far as Nashville is concerned. You can keep people down only so long as you can show that you're the top man. Once you ain't, then you're washed up.'

'You figured that Jed would be back with help in three, mebbe four, days. Any plans in the meantime, Marshal?'

'Some,' mused the other. 'You planted a thought in me a while back. Mebbe I ought to take another ride into Nashville and have a word with this editor feller. If I can get a State charge against Saunders, I'll feel a bit more sure of my ground.'

'You're crazy, Marshal. If you set foot in town, again, Foley'll git you fer sure. He won't let you slip through his fingers a second time.'

'That's a chance I've got to take. I figger if I go there after dark, I ought to be able to find out what I want to know and then hightail it outa Nashville before they know I'm there. I'm banking on this editor not being a friend of Saunders. He must have old documents there relating to the war.'

'Don't you think that Saunders would have seen to it that anything like that was destroyed a while ago? He isn't the kind of man who leaves anythin' to chance.'

'I'm banking that this time, he has. It's the only lead I have, and I've got to follow it up. Saunders won't be expecting me to go back into town. He'll figger that would be the action of a fool.'

'You're bein' a fool if you go through with this crazy idea of yours,' muttered the other. 'If you have to go, then let me come with you. At least I could—'

Bart shook his head. 'This is a job for one man only,' he said softly. 'Besides, we need every other man here, just in case Saunders and his men show up tonight.'

'Reckon you're right,' admitted the other reluctantly. He turned, then said grimly. 'I guess we'd better get those buzzards out there buried. A couple of our men were hit too, but they'll get by.'

That afternoon, a restlessness possessed Bart Nolan, a restlessness that made the hours drag. He had known that it might come to this, ever since he and Reva Benson had lit out of Nashville the previous night. There was a secret in Saunders' past that he had to find. Once he had that, he felt sure he would have everything he needed to hang the cattle baron.

Shortly before nightfall, he saddled the horse, then went back into the ranch. Reva Benson stood in front of him, her black hair glistening in the light of the fire. There was a look on her face and in her eyes which he had never seen before. 'You're still set on going into Nashville, Bart?' she said, making it more of a statement than a question. Her eyes searched his.

'I've got to, Reva,' he said tightly. 'This isn't something just for me now. It's for the whole of the valley, for Nashville. We have to get rid of Saunders before he can destroy everything. He's that kind of man, Reva. If he once gets it into his head that we've defeated him he'll turn that bunch of killers loose with orders to destroy everybody and everything. There is such a savage streak in him, his anger and hate is so great, that he'll take everything with him when he has to die.'

'And you think that going into Nashville, alone, tonight, will help to solve that?'

He shrugged. 'I've got to follow every lead I can. This man, Sefton, is my only hope right now. I've got to see him, make him talk. So he's scared, but you reckon he's a straight dealer. I think I can get him to tell me what I want to know.'

'And if he doesn't have the answers to your questions? What then? All of this will be for nothing.'

He said carefully: 'Saunders is so big a man that there has to be something in his past to explain all of this. He either got it by murder or some other means and until I know that, then I'm as much in the dark as the rest of you. That was what I was sent out here to discover. When help gets through from Bluff Creek, that will be the information they'll want before they make an arrest. Remember that Saunders has still got a lot of friends who'll back him to the hilt when the showdown comes.'

Her face softened. 'I guess you're right, Bart. It's just that—' She paused, twisting her hands together in front of her. Then she came close to him and lifted her face; and it held a lot of the old sweetness which he guessed it must have known before her father had been killed. For a long moment, he wished that he had known her in those days, but he knew, instinctively, that if everything went well, her eyes would laugh again and her lips would learn once more how to smile. He could do that much for her and the thought brought the strength and warmth back into his body. Outside, he heard the sharp neigh of the horse as it chomped impatiently on the bit.

She said softly: 'Bart, I wish you'd kiss me before you go.'

A little of the old hunger leapt up in him, a moment when nothing else counted for much and even Jeb Saunders was temporarily forgotten and then he released her and started for the door. He knew that he mustn't look back, that she would not expect him to do so, but she had looked pretty close to crying and that brought some of the saving anger back into his mind, anger against Jeb Saunders and all of the people in Nashville, who could not see where their destiny was leading them, or who were just too plumb scared to face up to this man who was hellbent on destroying them and everything they had built over the years.

The old cowhand was waiting for him, standing beside the horse. He said gruflly: 'Is there anything I can do for you, Marshal?'

'Yes, he said. 'Keep a watch over her. See that nothing happens to her until I get back.'

'I'll do that,' said the other very solemnly. 'She's my

friend too, you know. I worked for her father when he was alive. Now all that I want is to see her happy and those murderers brought to justice.'

He swung himself up into the saddle, sat for a moment looking down at the other, then said quietly: 'I'll be riding now. The sooner this night's work is done the better pleased I'll be.'

He touched spurs to his horse, lifted it to a steady gallop and headed eastwards, towards the moon which was just rising, touching, the tops of the trees with a brush of pale silver.

For a while he rode at full tilt, with the wind in his face, keeping his eyes and ears open for any sign of other riders on the trail. Then, as he approached the boundary of the Circle W, he swung left and headed northwards by a roundabout route which would take him across rough country, but well clear of the Lazy V ranch. In front of him, the land began to tilt upwards and there were tall pines that topped the low hills. The horse picked its way sure-footed along the dimly-lit trails. Very few riders ever came this way, he reflected, his keenly-trained eyes taking in every detail. At times, he was forced to slow his horse to a trot, but whenever the country permitted it, he gave it its head. The old hatred was still a leaping flame inside him and his right arm was stiff under the bandage.

Presently, he got out of the timber country and could look down into the valley. Nashville lay in the distance, about a mile and a half away to the south-east, a few lights still showing. The Lazy V ranch lay beyond the trees below him and although he probed the moonlight for any sign of riders, he saw nothing. A quiet, moonlit silence held the range for as far as the eye could see and he rode on into Nashville without passing a soul on the trail. A couple of hundred yards out of town, he reined the horse, slipped out of the saddle, shucked a box of shells into his pocket and then tethered the animal by the side of the trail, where there was grass to graze, and where he could find him in a hurry if he had to light out of Nashville with trouble on his heels.

He went the rest of the way on foot, his wide-brimmed hat pulled well down over his face. There were few people in the streets and the tents which the nesters had put up just on the outskirts were quiet. A brooding silence seemed to hang like a shroud over the whole town. Cautiously, he walked the wooden boardwalk, keeping well into the walls of the buildings. As he drew near the middle of the town, he picked out the sound of music from the saloon and voices from inside. It could be that Foley had another posse out, he reflected, or maybe the men were celebrating the fact that they were still alive after being jumped by the Circle W hands.

Carefully, he edged towards the closed doors of the saloon. Light spilled over them into the street. As he paused, there was a sudden shout from inside, then the doors swung open and a dark figure emerged into the night. Bart's hand closed over the butt of his sixer and he brought it instictively out of the holster in a blur of movement, then relaxed. The man swayed drunkenly in front of him for a moment, peering closely, shortsightedly at him in the manner of all drunks, then fell against the wall. He mumbled something under his breath as he went down, then his head dropped forward on to his chest and he began to snore loudly. Bart holstered his sixer, nudged the other with the toe of his boot, then moved on, lowering his head so that the light spilling out of the saloon passed over it.

He considered the odds which were stacked against him and smiled his bleak smile once more. He knew where the offices of the local paper were situated and made his way noiselessly towards them. A couple of cowhands came whooping through town, yelling and firing wildly into the air. Then they unsaddled in front of the saloon and barged inside. There was a brief flicker of light and then the doors swung shut once more and the street was in darkness with only the moonlight picking out the shadowy details.

There was a deep sense of urgency in Bart now. His brain was ice cool and he had temporarily forgotten the stiffness in his right arm. He unloosed the bandage and flexed his fingers as he paused in the darkness in front of the *Clarion* offices.

There were no lights in the building and when he tried the door it was locked as he had expected. There was a narrow opening at the side of the building and he padded along it. He was restless again and for that reason he was over-cautious. The quietness of the place reminded him that he was in the midst of his enemies, that he had only to be seen by one man for the news of his presence to be flashed all over town. Then the shooting would start and he couldn't hope to take on everyone in Nashville.

At the rear of the dark building, he paused, looked about him closely. His senses were straining intently but in spite of this, his eyes almost missed the dark shadow less than three feet away. The fact that there was someone else there, apparently on a similar errand to his own, seared through his mind like the scorch of a bullet. Instantly, he made up his mind. He couldn't use his gun. That would bring the whole of the hornet's nest down around his ears. This had to be done quickly and silently, without any fuss.

Easing the gun from his belt, he reversed it silently, until his fingers gripped the smooth steel of the barrel. Holding it like a club he crept forward, keeping close to the wall. In spite of his silence, the other must have sensed his presence for the figure whirled just as he came up behind it. The man threw up an arm over his head while

116

his other flashed down towards his gun belt. It was an instinctive move on Bart's part. The gun swung downwards in a short arc with all of his wiry strength behind the blow. The man gave a low moan, then fell forward on to his face. Bart leaned forward, felt the man's body with his hand, then holstered his gun. It had served its purpose. The other would not trouble him for a long time.

He found one of the windows at the back which hung open on a shattered latch and pushed it in with the flat of his hand. Moments later, he was inside, feeling his way forward in the darkness, narrowing his eyes to accustom them to the intense gloom. It was possible that Sefton was on the premises and if that was the case, the sooner he located him the better. Sefton was the one man who must have known Saunders in the old days. He had run the paper, even during the Civil War, for there had been reports brought out by him on the progress of the fighting.

'Sefton!' He called the other's name softly, then stood quite still, listening. The building was quiet. He called the editor's name once more and then, when he received no answer, went through the door in front of him and found himself in the printing room. A press stood in one corner and there were long shelves of ink and brushes ranged around the walls, with rolls of paper stacked in one corner. As his eyes became accustomed to the darkness, he realized that there was something wrong. Several of the bales of paper had been picked up and thrown into the middle of the floor; some of the lines of type were scattered over the shelves and over by the wide window, the papers which had been printed that day were piled high in a loose bunch by the wall. With an effort, he pulled himself together. What had happened here? Had Saunders been a little too clever for him; had the other guessed that, probably, sometime, he would come out here trying to get information – and being a careful and methodical man, Saunders had determined that every avenue for gaining that information should be closed to Bart Nolan.

It seemed the only possible answer. But what had happened to Sefton himself? Had he been forcibly removed to the Lazy V ranch, where he could give away nothing? Or had the same fate befallen him as had overtaken Joel Benson when he had become too big a menace to Jeb Saunders?

There was a rising sense of panic in his mind as he went through the house, room by room, occasionally calling Sefton's name softly, just in case the other had barricaded himself in somewhere and was waiting to cut loose with a gun as soon as anyone showed himself. But the entire house was silent and it was not until he reached the small room at the top of the stairs that he discovered the answer to his question.

Sefton lay face-downwards on the floor, just inside the door. He had a small pistol in his right hand, his fingers twined convulsively around it, but he had never had a chance to use it. There was still the smell of powder in the room and Bart guessed they were not long away. He crossed over to the window, looked out into the quiet street, but could see no one. The light was still shining in the saloon, but that was all. There was a sense of bleakness in his brain as he went back to where Sefton lay on the floor. There seemed to be something futile and pathetic in the way in which the other—

His thoughts gelled. The man on the floor moaned softly and tried to move. Swiftly, Bart went down on one knee, turned the other over gently. The gunshot wound was in his chest, just below the heart and he knew with a deeply ingrained instinct that for Sefton, even though he was not yet dead, the sands of time were swiftly running out. Pain moved in the man's face, twisted his lips like

118

those of a bear in a trap, until the teeth showed white in the shadow of his face.

'Saunders did this, didn't he?' said Bart swiftly. The other made no reply. Then his lips moved, but Bart had to bend close to him to pick out the words, spoken with a painful slowness, hesitant with the agony in the other's body.

'He – he said that I – I was too dangerous to live.' The other fought against the pain, conscious that his life was slipping away fast. He took a tight control over himself and his voice was a little stronger when he spoke again, moistening his lips with the tip of his tongue.

'I thought he'd keep his word. He swore I'd be all right so long as I didn't talk, and I never have. Not until now. I don't know who you are, Mister, but I've got a feelin' that you're not one of that bunch of crooks and killers.'

'I'm a Deputy United States Marshal,' said Bart tightly. 'I came here for the express purpose of smoking out this man Saunders and exposing him for what he is. A vicious murderer. But I need help to do it and I was told that you had some kind of evidence on him which could get him hung.'

'That's right. It all happened a long time ago. Six or seven years, I think.' He paused, seemed to weaken a little, then nodded his head slowly. 'After what he did tonight, I want to tell you everything about him. They came lookin' for that evidence, but I'd hidden it well. I don't think they found it. I kept it in the small safe in the wall of the printing room. It's downstairs, behind the picture. You'll find the combination in my pocket. They didn't get that. Those cuttings will tell you everything you want to know. They ought to give you enough to hang Saunders ten times over.'

Bart nodded. 'You'd better lie still while I try to get the doctor to take a look at you,' he said, forcing evenness into

119

his voice. 'He'll soon be able to patch you up as good as new. You'll live to fight Saunders to the death.'

Sefton shook his head wearily although the movement cost him much. 'There ain't no use lyin' to me now, Marshal. I know when it's time to hand in my chips. Besides, you'd only be risking your life if you tried to get the doctor across to see me. He's working for Saunders too.'

Bart said slowly: 'You're a strange man, Sefton. I'd never have figured you as a man who'd be scared of Saunders. I knew you weren't in his pay and yet you kept this secret of his all these years without once letting it out, knowing what he was doing to the rangeland and the town.'

Sefton licked his lips. For a moment, he seemed to have difficulty in speaking, then he found his voice and said hoarsely. 'It weren't fear of Saunders that made me keep my mouth shut about him, Marshal. Funny thing, now that I look back on it, I doubt whether I did the right thing, and I don't suppose she'd really understand why I did it.'

'She?' Bart raised his brows slightly. He squatted there in the darkness, looking down at the dying man in perplexity.

For a moment, there was the ghost of a smile on the editor's thinned lips. He nodded, swallowing. 'I had a wife once, Marshal. Mebbe you wouldn't believe it to look at an old cuss like me, but she was beautiful. She made it so that every day I could wake in the morning and think that it was goin' to be a good day ahead of me. I thought we had all the years to come, that I had everything that a man could ask out of life.'

'But Saunders came and—'

The other shook his head. For an instant, his body heaved as another spasm of pain lanced through him. Then it passed and he sank back, sighing, on to the floor again. 'It weren't Jeb Saunders. There was the war and towards the end, we had the Northerners, those goddarned Yankees in Nashville. They took everythin' they wanted, everythin' they could lay their dirty, thievin' hands on.' His voice shook momentarily with fury as the memory came flooding back into his mind. 'They took Grace and when they'd finished with her she would have been better off dead. She did die a month later. That was when I swore that I'd get even with the Yankees if it took me the rest of my life, that was why I kept that evidence and never told it to a soul. Much as I hated his guts, Jeb Saunders was a Southerner.' The ghost of a smile played around his lips for a moment. 'Funny how conflicting loyalties can ruin a man, Marshal. Having to choose between two evils like that.'

'Whatever you did, you've atoned for it now,' said Bart with feeling. 'I think your Grace will understand.' The other sighed and lay back. Presently, his eyes closed and he seemed to have fallen asleep, but after a little while a tremble seemed to pass through his body and when Bart reached out and felt his wrist, there was no pulse. He got slowly to his feet, stood for a moment looking down at the man who had, like Jeb Saunders, kept a secret for many years. Then he walked down the quiet stairs, into the printing room at the bottom and looked about for the picture on the wall. He found it easily, but at the back of it, he found something else. The door of the safe hung lopsided open and when he thrust his fingers inside, they encountered nothing but the bare metal walls of the safe.

For a long moment, he stood there, trying to think. It seemed incredible that Saunders could have beaten him like this. Sefton had seemed so sure that they had not found the safe that he had talked of everything but what that evidence was. Now Sefton was dead, the vital piece of evidence was gone, and Bart was right back where he had

121

started. The knowledge was almost more than he could bear. Frantically, he searched the room, trying to find something which might give him a clue but there was nothing. Twice, he was forced to stop in his desperate search as footsteps sounded on the boardwalk outside and he pressed himself tightly against the wall of the room, scarcely daring to breathe until the footsteps died away into the distance.

In the end, he was forced to acknowledge that the evidence he sought was no longer there, that Saunders or one of his men had discovered it and by now, it would be in Jeb Saunders's hands, possibly destroyed so that it was no longer a menace to him.

He let himself out of the rear of the house like a man walking in his sleep. His mind felt fuzzy and it was impossible to think clearly. He felt certain that there was something he had missed, but he could not remember what it was. Then he stumbled over the inert body of the man in the doorway, the man he had caught snooping around the house; and suddenly he knew what it was. The idea began as a small germ in the back of his mind, but built up to a certainty with a swiftness that surprised him. He thought: *This is the man who killed Sefton! I surprised him not going into the house, but coming out and if that's the case, then he still has that vital piece of evidence on him!*

Going down on one knee, he searched desperately through the man's pockets. Within minutes, he had found what he was looking for. In the moonlight, it was almost impossible to read what was printed on the two cuttings, but on one of them was a faded picture which, even in the dimness was easily recognizable. It was that of a man in the uniform of an officer of the Confederate Army and the face was that of Jeb Saunders, only the name beneath it said Colonel Bradley Weston.

Carefully, he folded it and placed it in his pocket, then

eased his way back along the narrow alley and into the main street. He walked down the boardwalk with a single mindedness of purpose that left him almost blind to everything that went on around him. He reached the edge of town and found the horse where he had left it. Loosening the reins, he swung himself stiffly into the saddle and side-reined the animal, turning its head swiftly away from Nashville. Thoughts were running around in his head like wild things, a few making a mixed-up kind of sense, but the other strange and new to him. That Jeb Saunders and Bradley Weston were one and the same man he did not doubt. But why had Saunders enlisted in the Confederate Army under a false identity. He knew that he would learn nothing more until he reached the Circle W ranch and examined these papers more closely.

He rode swiftly, consumed with the urgency which had been riding him all night. The edge of dawn was showing as he entered the Circle W spread and rode down out of the winding trail among the pines, into the meadowland. This first grey light made bleak, dark silhouettes of the trees, but there was a faint red flush on the crests of the mountains to the east where the hidden sun was laying its light on them.

Coming to the ranch, he saw that it was in darkness and there was a sudden chill finger on his heart as he dismounted and ran to the door. He shouldered through the door recklessly, calling Reva's name loudly and the place echoed his voice, threw the words mockingly back at him from the walls but he explored the house everywhere and Reva was not there. He knew that she would not have left of her own accord and for a moment, he stood contemplating that thought until a measure of patience came back to him and his first heady surge of angry fear gave way to one that was cold and purposeful and relentless.

SEVEN

OWLHOOT TRAIL

Bart's face was wooden as he went outside again. He was on the point of climbing back into the saddle when he noticed the marks of several horses in front of the corral. Going over, he went down on one knee and examined them closely, then paused as his sharp eyes spotted something else, the marks where a heavy body had been dragged over to the barn.

Swiftly, he went over, his gun sliding noiselessly from its holster. There was a mountain cat's restlessness about him as he kicked open the door, sharp wariness in his every movement as he edged inside. Then he holstered his gun as he saw the figure on the floor. The old cowpoke spat and muttered curses as Bart removed the gag and then cut the ropes which bound his arms and legs.

'What happened?' demanded Bart thinly. His hands were around the other's arms, fingers biting in with a steel-like strength.

'We was fooled,' complained the other bitterly. 'They played a coyote's trick on us and like goddarned fools, we fell for it.'

'Keep talking, but hurry,' snapped Bart. 'They've got

Miss Benson. Do you know where they've taken her?'

The other shook his head, rubbing his hands and legs to help restore the circulation. 'They pulled a raid in the north meadow, went for the steers and tried to stampede them. Ed and the boys went out after them. I stayed behind with Miss Reva. Then this killer Sutton and two of his men came at us. We held them off for an hour or so, but in the darkness, they managed to get inside the house. They must've knocked me cold with a rifle. When I came to I was out here, bound and gagged. I never saw what they did with Miss Reva. You don't reckon they've killed her?' For an instant, alarm and anger showed in the old-timer's face. He scrambled to his feet, then put his hand to his head.

'No. They won't have killed her – not yet.' Bart shook his head and tried to fight down the fear and panic in his mind. This was the last thing he had expected. 'They need her as a hostage. Saunders wouldn't be as big a fool as to kill her out of hand until he'd got what he wanted from us.'

'What're you goin' to do?'

'There's only one chance. Knowing Saunders, he'll have them taken to some out-of-the-way place, possibly somewheres to the south.'

'But that's desert country.' The other looked up at him in surprise.

'I know. But he'll figger that's the last place we'd go to look for her. There are plenty of abandoned mineworkings out there with one or two ghost-towns. Places they could hide out for days, but by that time, it'll be too late.'

'Then you don't stand a chance of finding her in time.' There was a bleak despair in the old-timer's voice.

'Not unless they've left a good trail and I can follow it. Once it hits the desert, it oughtn't to be too difficult. They won't be able to make good time either with Reva.'

'Want me to come along? I feel kinda guilty.'

'No. You'd better stay here. Some of the boys may come back and I'll need you to tell them what happened. But don't let any of them come after me. You'll need every man here in case they come again.'

The old-timer said huskily: 'I don't figger that you have much of a chance findin' those polecats in the desert, but I'll do anythin' you say.'

'Good. Keep a close watch here. If you can contact any of the other men, herd most of the steers towards the ranch where you can see them. Whatever you do, don't leave this place unguarded. They'll fire it as soon as they get the chance. Probably the only reason why they didn't do it the last time was that they wanted to get Reva away.'

The other said softly, 'I figger that you're aimin' to kill Sutton if you ever catch up with him. Am I right'?'

'You could be,' admitted Bart quietly.

'I guessed so. But be careful. He isn't like the others. He'll shoot you in the back and then claim it was self defence. He's as slimy as a rattlesnake and twice as deadly.'

'Thanks, I'll remember that.' Bart swung himself up into the saddle and led the horse slowly forward, keen eyes scanning the ground. The killers had made little attempt to hide their tracks and he was able to follow them clear across the meadowland. Then he hit the high ground, but kept himself well below the skyline just in case they had anyone watching the trail. The terrain changed gradually and in places, it was almost impossible to see the trail left by the Lazy V riders.

At a steady pace he rode over the rough ground, cutting into the desert country, the badlands, skirting wide chasms that plummeted downward into darkness, carving the ground into a blend of sunlight and shadow. Among the rocks, he rode quickly, keeping his eye on the trail ahead of him. It was not until he had been riding for more than two hours, that he came upon the slowly dying embers of the fire which had been lit in a narrow hollow among the boulders. The desert started less than a mile away and he guessed that the riders had stopped here for something to eat, before they had cut into the bad country. He stopped the horse and let it blow, while he examined the area for anything which might confirm his suspicions that Reva had been travelling with these men. But there was nothing definite there and when he remounted and started out along the trail again, he was still feeling uneasy in his mind. It was possible that he could have lost the trail some way back and this one that he was following so assiduously could have been made by some other party that had passed this way. By now, Reva and her captors could be miles away in the opposite direction. The thought almost broke him in half, but he pushed it out of his mind, dismissing it instantly. The chances of such a coincidence were very small. He forced himself to believe that he was on the right trail. He began to feel a little easier in his mind as he urged the horse forward, keeping a tight, short grip on the reins, guiding the mount between the boulders which lay strewn across the trail. The sun had risen higher now into the cloudless, blue-white heavens and the searing touch on his shoulders was like a finger of fire laid upon him.

It was a terrible trail, one which was rarely used since the other two had been opened further down in the valley, and the main trail into Nashville, further to the north, ran through lush, cool country. He watched constantly, ahead, each side, back in the direction he had come from which pursuit might come if he had been seen anywhere along the way. In places, the trail dropped down almost to the point where it joined the buttes trail; and then again, it would angle high up the side of the canyons, around steep bends to skirt the meandering sandstone walls of the bluffs.

Why anyone should have blazed a trail such as this, he did not know, although it probably dated from the early settler days and anyone riding through the country lower down was in danger of being attacked and scalped by the Osage or Choctaw Indians. As a result, they would grow to prefer discomfort and heat, to death.

By the time he had travelled for three hours and it was close on noon, every dusty, gritty, heat-seared fibre of his body had set up a mocking scream deep within him. In front of him, the buttes dropped away to where they faded into the desert, a terrible land of scrub and heat. He wondered how Reva would ever survive a journey such as this.

Pausing, he scanned the empty plain which lay ahead of him and narrowed his eyes against the harsh glare of the sun which seemed to have seared all of the colour out of the ground. At first, he could see nothing. Then, far below him, in the distance, was a cloud of dust, heading away from where he stood.

The sight sent a little thrill through him. He judged that the others were little more than four miles ahead of him. But his own mount was weary after the long night ride and the best he could hope for would be to keep them in sight until they reached their hiding place. He moved down the treacherous slope and into the desert only after the others had faded into the distance against the sun. It wouldn't do to be seen before he was ready. Here, in front of him, lay the ugly country. Few springs gushed up in this terrible, inhospitable terrain and the ground was arid, dotted here and there with the green-brown scrub which, in many places, was the only kind of vegetation to be seen.

Sand and sweat worked its way into the folds of his flesh, filling them with an itching ache that was both painful and irritating. The horse plodded steadily forward now, head down, the sun beating down on them, almost blinding them. There was no shade here, no place to escape that terrible, fiery glare. He rode in silence, speculating. As yet, he had no plan to put into action once he came up with the others. But that was a bridge he would have to cross when he came to it, he decided finally. There was no sense in filling his mind with problems now, slowing his reflexes down to danger point.

An hour later, he halted the horse in a sandy cut that ran at right-angles to the trail, beside a gummy water hole. The sun glow which filled the overhead dust was sickening and the heat waves seemed to be refracted from the desert around him so that they beat in endless waves against his face, forcing their way into his brain, even through the lowered lids. A few buzzards wheeled like tattered strips of black cloth against the cloudless blue of the sky.

He drank slowly, then stood up from the muddy water-hole, brushing his sleeve across his face to dash the sweat from his eyes. His cheeks were smeared with a coating of the yellow dust.

There was a dull sickness in the pit of his stomach as he started out again. Raising his eyes, he saw that the small cloud of dust was no longer there on the horizon. He shrugged. All he could do now was ride in the general direction in which he had last seen it and hope that he hadn't been seen and the others had either suddenly changed direction or were lying in wait for him. He hoped that he hadn't been seen. If he had, they might guess who he was and what his purpose would be when he caught up with them, and they might decide to kill Reva out of hand rather than let her escape them. He didn't know what Saunders' order had been on that point, but he guessed that, if the circumstances made it difficult for him, Sutton would shoot the girl and then try to fight his way out of trouble as best he could.

He felt jumpy as he pushed on into the uncompromising desert. The sun passed its zenith, but the terrible heat increased. The horse had slowed to a steady trot now and seemed unable to go any faster. Maybe he ought to have allowed the old-timer to accompany him, he thought dully, then shrugged the thought away. Two men would have kicked up a dust cloud that could have been seen for miles.

When he reached the far side of the desert country, there was no sign of Sutton and the others. But Bart knew from the past that there were plenty of old mine workings in this vicinity and he figured that Sutton knew of them too. They would have taken the girl into one of the abandoned shacks where they could keep her until Saunders showed up or sent fresh orders as to what they had to do with her. He walked the horse slowly forward, into the rugged terrain which bordered the desert. There was no sound around him but the faint cries of the buzzards wheeling overhead. He ignored them and concentrated all of his senses on listening for movement among the rocks. There might be a rifle trained on him at that very moment with an itchy trigger finger waiting to squeeze the trigger and blast him into eternity. The small hairs on the back of his neck began to crawl uncomfortably. But he knew that he had come this far and that he had to go on, no matter what might lie in store for him. He owed it to Reva Benson.

The sun went down suddenly and a deep purple flush spread rapidly from the east, covering everything, blotting out the long shadows into darkness. Bart's body felt tired and his thinking was sluggish. He turned over in his mind all that he remembered about this particular stretch of territory. In the old days. there had been a stage road running through these rocks, but it had long since been obliterated with time once the mine workings had run out and the men had drifted away. The war had finished it entirely and only the buzzards and men like Sutton ever came here now.

He climbed stiffly from the saddle as he entered the narrow ravine, where the old trail showed in places between high, rearing walls of stone and time-etched rock. Tethering the mount, he went forward on foot. His limbs and muscles ached with the strain of the day's ride, but a kind of excitement seemed to have taken hold of him, something that drove him on.

The first shack he reached he approached warily, his gun in his hand. There was no sound, but none of the killers would be doing much talking if they had seen him and knew he was on their trail. He scouted the hut carefully, then kicked the door open and went inside. It was empty, had been for years, with a thick layer of yellow dust lying undisturbed on the floor.

They had not come here. He moved on along the floor of the valley which had been cut through the rocks. Cool wind sifted down from the rocks and over his head the stars stood out, brilliant and numerous. He walked on, eyes alert, starting at every sudden sound or movement. Halfway along the valley he pondered on the wisdom of this move. He might need his horse in a hurry and having to leave it behind at the head of the valley could prove both troublesome and dangerous. But equally well, he doubted the wisdom of bringing it with him.

He began moving laterally along the face of the nearer slope, looking for a gentler pitch and in the end, he found one and made better progress. He wanted to jump these men before they had a chance to settle down for the night, when they were least expecting trouble.

Pausing often to keen the night, he was almost on top of them before he realized they were there. They had built themselves a fire in the open, on a rocky patch of open ground in front of the solitary, isolated shack. Two of them were seated in front of the fire, one on either side so that, by lifting their eyes, they could watch both directions. He frowned in the darkness, wondering where Reva and Sutton were, then decided that they were inside the shack. Obviously Sutton was taking no chances on the girl slipping away into the darkness, not that there was anywhere she could go. She could never make it back across that fearsome desert alone.

One of the two men was smoking and it was easy to pick out the red light of his quirly, a faint pin-point in the night. Very gently, Bart eased the gun back into his holster. This wasn't the time to make a move. Not with Sutton in the shack with the girl. He didn't doubt that the killer would use her as a shield if any trouble started. No – he wanted Sutton out in the open, where he could see him, once he started to make his play. The other two men looked like the ordinary run of cowpoke that one could meet up with on any ranch spread from Abilene to Dodge. They weren't killers in the strict sense of the word, but if the pay was right, and they were pushed hard enough, they would shoot. But he didn't think either of them would shoot an unarmed woman. It was Sutton he would have to watch when the shooting began.

He eased himself back into the shadow of the rocks and settled himself down to wait. There was a sense of drowsiness in his body which he fought off desperately. As far as these men were concerned, he needed all of his wits about him. ʼ

The minutes slipped by. The men at the fire talked together in low tones, but from that distance, it was impossible for him to pick out any of the conversation. He concentrated his attention on the door of the shack, waiting. After a while, it swung open and Reva appeared. Her clothing was dust-streaked and bedraggled and she looked almost dead on her feet. He saw that they had not harmed her, but Sutton thrust her roughly in front of him, so that she stumbled on the rocks and almost fell full length in front of the fire.

One of the men, raising his voice a little so that it carried to Bart, said harshly: 'Ain't no call to treat her like that, Sutton.'

'Shut your lip,' snarled the other viciously. 'If she had her way, we'd all be swinging from the end of a rope. Remember that, Jackson. You, too, Wade. Don't waste any of your pity on Joel Benson's daughter. She's one of the same breed.'

He thrust at the girl once more and laughed harshly. With an effort, Bart kept his hand away from the gun in his belt and tightened his fingers until they hurt. The two men fell silent and one of them stirred the iron pot over the fire sullenly. He sat with his head bowed and from his appearance, Bart judged that his heart wasn't in the job he had been forced to do. The knowledge brought a little hope into his heart. Sutton was the dangerous man. If he could drop him, he doubted whether the other two men would fight, especially if he could somehow give the impression that they were surrounded and outnumbered.

He edged closer, keeping into the cover of the rocks. Soon, he was close enough to be able to overhear them. 'You figger that he'll be following us once he finds out what has happened?' asked the man, Wade.

'Could be,' muttered Sutton surlily. 'If only we'd found him there too, when we drew off that other crowd, this might not have been necessary. But if he does follow us, and I reckon our trail ought to be clear enough across that goddarned desert, then we'll be ready for him. You both know what to do?'

'Sure,' broke in the other man. He stuffed a spoonful of food into his mouth and chewed on it slowly. 'We'll be up there among the rocks, while you stay in the hut with the girl. Once he makes his play for you, we get him from there.'

'That's right. And I don't want any mistakes. As far as this man Nolan is concerned, there've been too many mistakes in the past and Saunders don't like it. He's getting worried. We don't know where he went last night. He could have doubled back into town and that might be bad for all of us. He knows too much.'

'What if he comes with the rest of the Circle W men? We couldn't take on the whole gang.'

'He won't. I know Nolan. He'll come hightailing it out here as soon as he picks up our trail.'

'When do you figger he'll come?'

'How the hell should I know.' The other's voice sounded irritated and a little jittery. Among the rocks, Nolan eased himself into a more comfortable position. He felt a little more sure of himself now. Two things were immediately obvious. They had not seen him trailing them, even though they expected him to show up; and it was plain that something was worrying Sutton. He wasn't as confident as when Bart had last seen him. He was nervous, jumpy and kept throwing swift glances into the rocks all around him.

'You lookin' fer somethin', Sutton?' asked Wade after a while, noticing the other's movements. 'Do you figger he might have overtaken us already?'

Sutton made an ungainly shape seated by the fire. He made a sharp hunching movement with his shoulders, then shook his head, as if he had suddenly reached a decision within himself. 'Shucks, no. He ain't here yet. Probably he'll hole up in some gopher hole on the way here. I reckon we can give him until sun-up. But we'll be ready for him just in case.' He jerked his thumb towards the rocks on either side of the trail. 'As soon as you've eaten, git up there and take your positions. But remember what I told you. I don't want him dead when you take him. Shoot him in the legs. I want to see his face before he dies.'

There was a note of pure hatred in the other's voice that sent the little shiver of nameless fear tracing a path along Bart's spine. But now he knew their plans, he could make his own accordingly. The fact that the three men would be split up simplified matters quite considerably.

Bart's hope now was, that if he could take the pair of men one at a time, and deal with them silently, he might be able to surprise Sutton before he had a chance to harm Reva. It was the only chance he had, and he allowed his mind to dwell on it running over all of the possibilities while he waited for the party by the fire to break up. When they did, they moved exactly as he had anticipated.

Wade took the side on which he lay, clambering noisily into the rocks. Several times, Bart heard the metallic clatter as his sixes struck the rocky side of the narrow gulch up which he climbed. There was no sign of the other man and he guessed that he was somewhere on the other rocky face of the canyon. Sutton was still sitting by the fire with the girl.

Very carefully, Bart made his way up the rocks, snaking along narrow defiles which caught his eyes. He moved like a cat in spite of the stiffness in his limbs, but several times he was forced to pause for breath. These men had been able to rest up for several hours before he had caught up with them. They were a lot fresher than he was and he hoped that this would not tell on him when the time for instant action came. One wrong sound from either man would warn Sutton and that could mean the end for the girl. He came out of the rocks some distance above the point where he judged Wade to have taken up his position and a moment later, peering carefully over the rocks, he spotted the cowhand, squatting in a small hollow with his rifle rested on the ledge in front of him. He had chosen the spot with care for it commanded an excellent view along the canyon and from there, he would be able to see any movement for the best part of two hundred yards. Bart shivered slightly as he realized what might have happened, what would certainly have happened, if he hadn't been close enough to overhear their plan and see what they intended to do. One shot from that rifle through his leg and he would stand little chance of fighting three armed men.

He debated how to take this man. If he used his sixer as a club, even that slight sound might give him away. In the end, he slithered soundlessly down the defile until he was right behind the other. Pushing the barrel of his Colt hard into the man's back he whispered softly: 'Relax, Wade. One sound from you and this gun goes off.'

He felt the other stiffen but the man made no sound. 'That's better. I've got no quarrel with you. Only with Sutton, but I aim to get him. If you want to die right here, try for your gun.'

The other moved his hands slowly away from the rifle. Reaching down, Bart pulled the guns from the other's holsters, stuffed them carefully into his belt, then prodded the man to his feet. 'Now move very quietly back into the rocks. Walk in front of me and remember that I've got a very itchy trigger finger.'

Without a sound, the man walked in front of him, picking his way cautiously through the boulders, obviously valuing his life sufficiently to do as he was told. When he judged that they were well away from the shack and that sound would not carry back to Sutton, Bart swiftly reversed his gun and brought the butt crashing down on the back of the other's head. The man slumped tiredly forward into the rocks and lay still. Swiftly, Bart made his way back to the trail. There was no sound over the canyon.

The second man, on the far side of the trail was more wary than the first. Whether he had heard something and it had made him doubly suspicious or not, it was impossible for Bart to tell. But he kept twisting his head, peering in every direction, even behind him at times, eyes flicking from side to side, warily, probing every shadow around him for anything that moved. Worse still, he held his sixer in his right hand, the rifle propped against a rock in front of him.

There was little time to think. Instinctively, Bart slithered over the rocks, pausing at times as the other turned sharply and seemed to stare right through him, while Bart held his breath, ready to shoot if he had to. Very carefully, he circled the watching man, came to within three feet of him and remained there for a moment crouched ready to spring.

Then, far down the trail, there was a sudden sound. He recognized it instantly, the snicker of his horse which he had tethered to the rocks. Something, possibly a mountain cat on the prowl had disturbed the beast. He saw, out of the corner of his eye, the man in front of him jerk upright, every muscle of his body taut. For a moment, the man hesitated, then he plunged his sixer back into its holster, leaned forward and grabbed at the rifle.

It was the chance Bart had been waiting for. Gliding smoothly forward, he came up behind the other, a rearing shadow, the gunpoint in the small of the man's back before he realized his presence.

'If you want to stay alive, keep your mouth shut and do as I tell you,' he hissed. For a moment, he thought that the other would try to swing and use his rifle, then as he tightened his finger on the trigger, the man suddenly relaxed. Bart nodded to himself, satisfied. He had judged both of these sidekicks well. They were not going to get themselves killed just to protect Sutton.

'Lower that rifle and then back into the rocks,' he ordered.

The man obeyed and within minutes, he was unconscious among the boulders in company with his companion.

Bart emptied his lungs in a sudden sigh. So far, everything had gone without a hitch, but now came the tricky part. He slithered down the rocks and circled around the shack. There was a flickering light showing inside and he guessed that Sutton had found an old paraffin lamp somewhere and had lit it. So far, the other gave no sign that he had heard the sharp snicker of the horse along the canyon. Bart had hoped that he would have come out to investigate, but in this he was disappointed. Either Sutton had not heard it, or he was lying in wait inside the shack, waiting for his two sidekicks to take care of Bart before he moved in.

The old shack stood there in the moonlight with just a few boulders spread in front of it and the four horses tethered a little way back among the rocks. Bart walked slowly forward and moistened his lips. He went to the side of the hut where there were no windows and stood there for a long moment, listening. Then he moved along the wall until he reached one of the windows. Very carefully, he peered inside.

Sutton stood there with his back to him. Reva sat in a broken-down chair near the table. Her hands were tied in front of her and there was a smear of blood on her forehead. She looked tired and beaten. Slowly, an intense anger filling him, Bart slid the guns from their holsters, noticed that the door was hanging slightly ajar, and went towards it. He paused for a moment in front of it and heard the girl's voice say thickly:

'You'll never get away with this, Sutton. Even if you kill me, others will come into the valley and run you and

Saunders down. Then they'll hang you like you tried to hang Bart Nolan.'

'Nobody's goin' to do any hangin' like that,' snapped Sutton. His voice was hard. 'And as for Nolan, he's as good as dead right now. He'll be following us, probably a couple of miles behind. We deliberately left a trail that a blind man could've followed. He won't miss it and when he comes blunderin' into this valley, we'll have our sport with him. This time, he ain't goin' to die easy.'

'You think he'll be fool enough to walk into a trap like that.' There was scorn in Reva Benson's tone now.

'He'll come and when he does—'

Sutton had no time for any more. With a savage thrust of his foot, Bart kicked open the door and strode into the room. Sutton swung round savagely at the sudden intrusion, then his square face twisted into the fighting snarl of a cornered rat as his hands flashed down towards his guns. Both of Bart's sixes blasted at the same time. Sutton staggered back, caught off his balance, the Colts shot from his hands. His bulging eyes stared hatred at Bart as he came up against the wall and looked down at his smashed hands, the blood beginning to well from them, where the slugs had hammered into his fingers.

'This is the end for you, Sutton,' gritted Bart thinly. He motioned the killer across the room. 'I'd kill you right where you stand, but I may need your testimony when we come to hang Jeb Saunders.'

Sutton's lips twisted back into a thin smile. 'You figgerin' on takin' me back into Nashville?' he muttered.

'That's right,' Bart nodded. 'But by the time we get back, I reckon that we'll find that Jeb Saunders is no longer boss of the cattle range, or of Nashville. His days are numbered, whether he likes it or not.'

Sutton seemed to regain control of himself. 'You've got nothin' on Saunders that will stand up in court,' he snarled. 'And you know it. You're bluffin', Nolan. Besides, as soon as you walk out of this shack one of my men will drop you from the rocks. How they let you slip by, I don't know. But they won't let you get out alive, that much is certain.'

It was Bart's turn to shake his head. He caught the girl's look of apprehension, then smiled over the table at her. 'Those two men of yours won't be doin' any shooting for quite a while,' he said calmly. 'They weren't exactly asleep at their posts, but they never figgered on lookin' behind them. They're both asleep now and I doubt whether either of them will wake up much before dawn and even then they won't be in any condition to fight.' He noticed the sudden slump of the killer's shoulders and knew that he had made his point. 'You should never discuss your plans when your enemy might be within earshot,' he said tightly. 'Seems I wasn't as far behind you as you'd figgered.'

'You've still got to get us back to Nashville,' hissed the other thinly. 'And that ain't goin' to be so easy. It's the best part of a day's journey over that blistering hell of a desert. And even when you do get back, you'll have to face Saunders.'

'Saunders is finished. I have all of the evidence I need to get him hung. Your little plan to kill Sefton, the editor, didn't quite work out the way you planned it. Oh, sure, you killed him all right, but the killer you sent after him didn't get away with the evidence. I have it with me right now.' His voice sharpened as he prodded Sutton with the Colt. 'Untie Miss Benson and be very careful what you do. I don't need your testimony all that bad that I wouldn't shoot you if you tried any tricks.'

While the girl chafed her wrists, Bart ordered Sutton to collect two of the horses and bring them over to the shack. 'Now mount,' he ordered. 'And keep your hands on the saddle where I can see 'em.'

140

Getting his own mount, he climbed up into the saddle, waiting until the girl was ready on her own horse, before pulling out. The horses were still tired, but he was determined to travel as far as possible over the desert before dawn.

When dawn broke, they were in the middle of the badlands, pushing their way through the knee-high scrub. Occasionally, Bart threw a swift glance over his shoulder but there was no sign of pursuit from either of the two men he had knocked cold among the rocks. He guessed that as soon as they came round, they would saddle up their horses and head south for the Rio and across the border into New Mexico. Things were going to break as far as Saunders was concerned and rats like that wanted no part of it when the chips were cashed in and things started to go against them. He wondered how many more of the rats would leave once they heard that Saunders was finished. He doubted whether the cattle baron could count on more than a dozen of his hired killers who might stand by him. But everything seemed now to depend upon the Circle W foreman. He ought to have reached Bluff Creek the previous day if he had been pushing his mount to the limit; and Bart knew that the Federal Marshal would not waste any time once he got that report. He would act instantly, probably asking for troops.

As they rode, the sun climbed higher towards the zenith and the intolerable heat increased. Bart felt sick and stunned by it as it shocked up off the yellow scrub around them and time and time again, his head jerked forward on to his chest, his eyes lidding and closing with the weariness that flooded over him. Two nights and days without sleep were beginning to take their toll of him; but he knew that, whatever happened, he had to keep an eye on Sutton. Although the other's hands were securely lashed together in front of him, he was still as cunning as a mountain cat

141

and would turn on him at the first opportunity.

But Sutton did not make his play until they were within sight of the rocky buttes and the trail had narrowed out of the desert and was beginning to climb slowly, winding up into the rocks. In places, they had to ride in single file and Bart made the killer ride first where he could keep an eye on him. As they were negotiating a narrow, precarious ledge of rock the girl's mount suddenly stumbled, fought momentarily for its balance, and in spite of himself Bart's attention was dragged away from Sutton for that brief fraction of a second which was all that the killer needed.

He dug his spurs into the horse's flanks so that it leapt forward in a sudden convulsive jerk. Then he was gone, around the sharply-angled bend in the trail. Bart could hear the hoofbeats thundering away into the distance as he rode instinctively forward to help the girl.

Her horse had lamed itself when it had stumbled and one glance was enough to tell Bart that it could go no further. 'Better get down and ride up with me,' he said thinly.

'Don't you think you ought to go after Sutton,' she asked anxiously. 'If he gets back to Nashville, he'll warn Saunders. Then you won't stand much of a chance. They'll be waiting for you along the trail when you ride in.'

'That's a chance I'll have to take,' he said quietly. 'You're my first concern at the moment. Although I must admit, I'm wishing that I had shot him when I had the chance.'

He helped Reva up into the saddle, then pulled out his gun and shot the other horse, putting it quickly out of its agony. It would have stood very little chance of survival in that terrible country and he knew that, sooner or later, the mountain cats would pick up its trail and it was better that he should shoot it than allow it to be pulled to pieces by them.

Slowly, they wound their way along the mountain trail, over Buzzard's Ridge until they were crossing the final ridge before dropping down into the valley. Bart rode cautiously, eyes alert, all of the fatigue washed from his body by the knowledge that Sutton was somewhere ahead of them, riding hell for leather into Nashville bringing Saunders the news that not only was Bart Nolan still alive, but that he had rescued Reva Benson and had damning evidence with which to destroy him.

It was possible that Sutton might be lying in wait for him somewhere along the trail, that he had managed to untie his hands and would be smarting for revenge against the man who had made him look such a fool. But a mile further on, all doubts as to Sutton's whereabouts were stilled. They found Sutton and his horse lying among the rocks on the valley floor, within a few yards of each other. It was not difficult to see what had happened. In his desire to get away, Sutton had ridden his horse far too hard and having his hands tied, had been unable to guide the animal with the reins. Somewhere along that rock-strewn and treacherous trail which was only a couple of feet wide in many places, the horse had lost its footing, plunging over the cliff face, taking its rider with it. Bart dismounted and moved closer to take a better look. Sutton must have been killed instantly, he reflected. No man could have survived a fall such as that – over two hundred feet on to solid rock – and lived for long. He went through the killer's pockets, but found nothing apart from a wad of tobacco and a bill carrying his picture, with the wanted sign beneath it.

Bart smiled bleakly, then rose to his feet and went back to where Reva sat watching him, wide-eyed.

'Dead,' he said briefly. 'That's one more killer we won't have to worry about when the showdown comes. Maybe it's better that way. I doubt whether Saunders would have been any easier on him once he learned that he'd failed to hold you back there. Jeb Saunders isn't the kind of man who tolerates failure.'

He swung himself up behind her again, turned the horse's head in the direction of Nashville. There was still some unfinished business to do before Saunders was finished and there was the start of a better life for everyone in the town.

By noon, they had crossed from the mountainous country on to the lower trail which wound through the lush meadowland and for the first time since he had hit this territory, in spite of the weariness which was coming back into his body, Bart had the feeling that his mission was almost at a close, that very soon now, the turning point would come.

EIGHT

THE TALL MEN RIDING

At sunset, Bart Nolan and Reva Benson came to the Circle W ranch and behind them lay a long day's hard riding which had taxed the endurance of them both, for the valley which they had travelled stretched for close on twenty miles to the buttes and the yellow desert. Their shadows were long as they rode towards the ranch-house and dismounted in front of the long, low building. The rest of the hands came out to meet them and Bart breathed a sigh of relief as he saw that nothing seemed to have happened while he had been away.

'So he got you back safe and sound, Miss Reva,' said the old-timer. 'What happened to that rattlesnake, Sutton?'

'He's dead,' said Bart briefly. 'Tried to outrun us when Miss Reva's horse slipped on one of the mountain trails, but he didn't make it far. Horse must have gone over the side and they fell nearly a coupla hundred feet into the valley.'

The other nodded his head slowly and there was a hard glitter in his deep-set eyes. 'That's justice, I reckon,' he said thoughtfully. 'Just the sort of way a polecat like that oughta die. Can't say there'll be many who'll miss him.'

They went into the house and Bart noticed that the windows and doors were all barricaded in preparation for any attack the Lazy V riders might make on the place. Rifles were stacked in the corners of the room.

'Any sign of Jed and the others?'

'Nothin' so fer. We reckoned he ought to have got back today, or perhaps tomorrow morning. You figger he may have run into some kinda trouble out there? A lot could happen to a man betwen here and Bluff Creek.'

'I know. That's what's bin worryin' me all day.' He lowered himself into one of the chairs and let the weariness seep through his bones. His body had taken quite a beating one way or another during the past few days, he reminisced. But all they needed now was a bit of luck and this could be finished, quickly and decisively, one way or the other. Now, everything depended upon one thing. Whether the troopers or Saunders' men got to the Circle W ranch first.

'You look as though you could sleep the clock round,' said Reva. 'Don't you think you ought to get some sleep. All of the men are here now. They'll be ready if trouble comes. Saunders and his hired killers won't find it easy to take us by surprise again.'

'Reckon you could be right at that,' he agreed. His mind was working sluggishly and his reflexes were slow. He knew that he would find it difficult to handle a gun when the time came unless he could rid himself of some of this weariness and stiffness. True, there was no telling what Saunders was doing at that moment. He might still have it figured that Sutton was holding Reva at the old mine workings to the south and if he still thought that, he might hold his hand for a little while, hoping to catch two birds with one shot. Reva and Bart himself. They were the two people that Saunders feared the most; the two people who still stood between him and his dream of an empire here in Nashville. He had to get rid of them decisively and yet not too conspiciously, otherwise there might be more trouble. He leaned back in the chair and closed his eyes. All in all, things seemed to be turning in Bart's favour. Three of the most feared killers in the west were dead, four if he included Ed Wiley.

And when your enemy was dead, that was the end of him and the end of everything as far as he was concerned. It was with this comforting thought in his mind that Bart remained true to his word and slept the clock around. When he was roused, the sunlight was glinting in through the barricaded windows and it was late morning. The sound of hoofbeats outside brought him fully awake and he was at the nearby window, the sixes in his hands, before the solitary rider had drawn rein in front of the ranch.

Reva was beside him in an instant, peering out over his shoulder, then she relaxed. 'It's one of my men,' she said shortly. 'I have two watching the fence to the east. I figured that when Saunders came, he'd have enough men to ride in quite openly and that's the way he'd come. Looks like trouble.'

They went outside. The man was sliding quickly from his horse, the sweat glistening on the animal's flanks testifying to the way in which he had punished it across country.

'A party of men headed this way,' said the other hurriedly. 'We spotted them from the east fence. Too far away along the trail to tell how many there were, but it looked a mighty big party to me. Fifty or sixty, I reckon.'

'Could you make out who they were?' snapped Bart tensely. He felt the sinking stab of defeat in his mind. No matter how well they fought or barricaded the ranch, they couldn't hope to hold out against as large a force as that.

147

The other shook his head. 'Couldn't tell, Marshal. They were headed this way fast. I rode on ahead of Carter and Fothergill to give the warning. They'll be about two miles behind me.'

'Get all of the men together,' snapped Bart tightly. 'You're sure we have all of the guns inside the ranch, Reva?'

She nodded. Her eyes were clouded, he saw, and there was a look of deep concern on her regular features, but nothing of fear. 'Yes, Bart, they're all there.'

'Then let's get inside. This looks as if it's going to be a fight to the finish. Saunders, if those are his men, really means business this time.'

'You figure he knows that we're here?' she asked as they went back into the ranch.

'He could,' nodded Bart. 'Those two guards I left behind in the rocks back at the mine workings. They could have ridden hell for leather to warn him. They wouldn't know what had happened to Sutton, only that we'd taken him with us. That might be the one thing which could have forced his hand. In the right circumstances, Sutton might talk, might blow the whole tale. He can't know that Sutton is dead, so he's got to make sure of us.' His voice was tight and grim as he looked around the room. Most of the men were inside now and had taken up their positions by the windows and doors. Bart knew that every other room in the ranch was also filled with waiting, watching men; and he also knew that it would be a one-sided fight once those men arrived.

For a long while, there was silence over the rangeland. Then, in the distance, Bart heard the thunder of hoofs and looking out to the east, saw the dust of their coming. There was a tightness in his body which he couldn't quite force away and the fingers which gripped his sixes were flexed almost convulsively.

'Let them get within range before you open fire,' he called to the others. 'We haven't got any ammunition to waste. If I know Saunders, he'll call them down well out of range and then spread them out to encircle the place.'

Gently, he eased himself forward so that he could watch the approach of the oncoming men, riders and horses virtually hidden in the dust cloud which swirled about them, kicked up by the pounding hoofs, a dust cloud which was slow to settle.

He waited for the man in front to halt the riders, call them down from the saddle and come the rest of the way on foot so that they presented difficult targets, but instead, the party continued to ride forward. Bart squinted his eyes against the glare of the sun and tried to pick out details. He knew that there was something here which he did not quite understand and then he looked again and the sudden reality rose up and crowded the room.

'Hold your fire, men!' he yelled sharply. 'That ain't the Saunders bunch. Those are troopers!'

They went out then, into the bright sunlight and Bart knew that his mission was now almost over. These were men who had fought in the war just past and who now were stationed throughout the territory riding the rough, untamed country, keeping law and order along the frontier. With them rode Jed and another man, sitting tall in the saddle, a broad-shouldered, grey-haired man who grinned down at Bart and when he slipped from the saddle, the slight movement brushed back his vest and the yellow sunlight glittered briefly on the badge thus revealed. The shield-shaped badge of a United States federal marshal, like that which Bart carried hidden in his riding boot.

'Got here as soon as I could, after I'd picked up a little help, Bart,' he said, coming towards them. He gripped Bart's hand in a tight, firm hold. 'This is Captain Madison of the Fifth Cavalry. He's been detailed to give us all the help we need. From what I heard of this man Saunders, we're going to need every man here.'

'He'll fight to the finish, I'm convinced of that,' said Bart. 'He knows what's waiting for him if he's ever taken alive.'

'You said that you hoped to get hold of some evidence which could clinch the case against him, Bart. Did you get it?'

Bart dug into his pocket, pulled out the folded newspaper clippings and handed them over to the other. The grey-haired man stared down at them, then read through them slowly. Finally, he looked up. 'This is more than enough to hang him, Bart.' He turned to the Captain. 'I think this might interest you, Captain Madison. It could answer some of the questions which have been puzzling your superiors since the war ended.'

The captain took the papers and Reva Benson asked: 'What it is, Bart? What are those papers?'

Bart smiled thinly. 'It's a long story, Reva,' he said quietly. 'But it seems that Jeb Saunders entered the Confederate Army under the name of Bradley Weston. Seems he served with distinction during the first year of the war and soon became promoted to the rank of Colonel.'

'But why use a different name?' The girl turned a curious look on him.

'Because he meant to get far more out of the army than he ever put into it. Seven months before the war finished, he deserted in the face of the enemy and if the authorities had found him, he would have been court-martialled and shot for cowardice. But Saunders was a little too clever for them. About the time of his desertion, a supply wagon carrying currency for the Northern Armies was captured by a patrol of the Confederates and was being taken back to their lines. Saunders and a band of cut-throats ambushed the men and the wagon, killed them all and took the money. There was close on a hundred thousand dollars in that wagon. Saunders got it all, killed the men with him and went into hiding in the desert to the south of here. When the war was over, he came back to the Lazy V and built up the herd with the money he had stolen.'

'That's right,' continued Captain Madison grimly. 'Mind if I keep these papers, Bart?'

Bart shook his head. 'If they'll help to hang Saunders and the other crooks with him, keep them by all means.' The captain pushed them into the pocket of his tunic, his face grim. 'That was something which had been puzzling us for a long time,' he agreed. 'It was unfortunate for Saunders that there was one picture of him while he was serving under the name of Bradley Weston. How this man, Sefton, got hold of it, I don't suppose we'll ever know. It's also a pity that he was so bitter against the North even after it was all over. Otherwise, all of this might have been prevented.'

Bart said quietly: 'What do you figger on doin' now, Captain?'

'We're here to take him back to Bluff Creek for trial. But I gather from what you say, that this will have to be handled like a small army operation. We passed the Lazy V ranch on the way here and it looked as if every crooked gambler and gunslammer in the country was heading in that direction. Mebbe we ought to have hit them then, but we had to be sure that you had this evidence. Now that we have it, I reckon we'd better ride once we've rested our horses.'

'It ain't goin' to be easy to smoke them out of that place,' warned Bart. 'I've been there and I know. They can turn it into a fortress and with all of those guns at his command, you'll have to prise him loose.'

'We'll get him,' declared the other confidently. 'He looked around at the rest of the men from the Circle W. 'I

151

know some of you men have old scores to settle with Jeb Saunders and his men. I'll be glad to have any of you with me when we ride.'

Bart saw the hard light which gleamed in the eyes of the waiting men and knew what was coming.

'We'll throw in with you, Captain,' said Jed. 'I've been waiting fer this all my life. After what they did to Joel Benson, none of 'em deserve to live. They whipped him while they dragged him through Nashville, then took him out and shot him in the back.'

It was later that afternoon when they rode out of the Circle W range and headed for the Lazy V. A small detachment of the troops went on into Nashville to arrest Sheriff Foley and any other crooked deputies who might be there. Bart doubted if there would be many of them in town. Saunders would have given the orders by now and every available man who have been told to report to the ranch. The showdown was here and he would need every crooked gambler and gunman he could get.

There was little said in the long ride to the Saunders ranch. The men were hard-faced and stoney-eyed, lips hot, their nostrils pinched and white with the seething anger that they were holding in check. Some fingered their guns absently, others stared straight ahead, eyes alert for trouble, but knowing by some instinct that they would meet none of the Lazy V hands until they reached the ranch. Saunders would be staking everything on this one gun battle with the law. If he lost, then his whole empire would fall about him like a pack of cards. If he won, it would mean the end of law and order in that neck of the territory for some time to come.

The riders did not spare their horses. There were still four or five hours of daylight left and the sun was still high as they pounded the trail. In a surprisingly short time, they came to the turn-off into the Lazy V spread and the captain ordered the men to spread out as they approached the entrance to the ranch, ready for trouble. Bart was with the captain when they rode up to the gate set in the wire. For a moment the captain hesitated, then he pulled out his revolver and deliberately blasted the lock off so that it fell in jangled ruin on to the ground. Then he nudged his horse forward, pushing the gate open. The others followed through, close on their heels.

Shading his eyes, Bart glanced in the direction of the ranch. The corral was empty. The place seemed deserted too. But that was, he knew, only an outside impression. In his mind's eye, he could visualise the men crouched down behind the windows, their rifles pointed towards them, ready to open fire as soon as they rode within killing distance.

'He's holed up all right, Captain,' said Bart grimly. 'Just as I fingered he would be. Probably got some men in the barn too. You'd better keep your eye on it in case they try to rush us from that direction.'

The other nodded grimly to show that he understood. He signalled his men forward, forming them out into a long line, the ends of which began to circle slowly, the men spreading out as they rode. Bart loosened his sixes. He knew that, with their rifles, the men inside the ranch would have a longer range and would be able to open fire on them before they, themselves, could get within range. He rode steadily forward beside the captain, sitting easily in his saddle, but ready to whip his body into instant action at the first sign of trouble.

'Are you in there, Saunders?' yelled the captain loudly. There was a pause and then the other's voice came back from one of the windows.

'I'm here, trooper. I'd advise you to get off my land before I blast you.'

'You don't stand a chance. The ranch is completely

surrounded and we're coming in if you don't surrender. That goes for the men with you, too.'

Jeb Saunders laughed harshly and the sound of it echoed out into the yard. 'If you figger you can get me, Captain, then you're welcome to come and try.' He punctuated his words with a rifle shot that kicked dirt a few yards in front of the Captain's horse. The other did not flinch.

'This is your last warning, Saunders. You've come to the end of the trail now. With the evidence we have, you'll hang once you're taken. That goes for most of your men too.'

'Then we don't seem to have any choice, do we?' sneered the other. He was keeping himself well hidden behind one of the windows and Bart tried to figure out which direction his voice came from, but it was impossible. 'You've got plenty of nerve coming here like this, Captain. I fought your kind in the war and I know just what you're like, a lot of yeller-livered, loud-mouthed cowards.'

Bart saw the captain's face whiten and knew the strain which the other was imposing on himself to keep calm. Then he shouted: 'You ain't foolin' anybody, Saunders. And as for being a coward, mebbe the name Bradley Weston means somethin' to you. You see, we know all about the man who deserted and then killed his comrades once they'd stolen a wagon full of Yankee currency. You killed Sefton because you figgered he might talk and let out your little secret, only you hadn't figgered on somebody happenin' along at the same time. Somebody who got a hold of that evidence.'

There was a pause, then Saunders's voice, hard and tight with fury yelled: 'God blast you, Nolan. I might have figured it would have been you. But you won't live to make any more trouble for me. If I've got to go, I'll take you with me.'

154

There was the sharp crack of another rifle shot and Bart threw himself instinctively sideways in the saddle as the slug hummed by, close to his head. He turned sharply to the captain.

'We're getting nowhere with this parleyin', Captain. I say we'd better go in there and smoke 'em out.'

'Reckon you're right, admitted the other. 'I guess I knew that Saunders would never meet any terms I could offer and he's too clever a man to fall for any promises I could make to get him out into the open.' He rode back to the waiting men and signalled them forward. The troopers moved almost as one man, slipping from their horses and running forward through the tall grass, heads low, circling the ranch house. From the barn came a storm of fire as they swung in close and Bart saw two men fall as the slugs poured among them.

'I'll take the rest of the men and we'll attack from the rear,' he yelled to the captain. Before the other could nod or argue, he had motioned the men from their mounts and they were snaking towards the side of the ranch, cutting through the meadow towards the cookshack. Time passed slowly as they edged their way forward. For a long while, there was no sound or movement from that side of the house, then as they ran forward, a gun barked. Dust spurted up just in front of Bart Nolan.

'No further, lawman,' yelled a voice which he didn't recognize. 'The next slug will be in your heart.'

Bart lunged to the side, hit the ground and rolled over twice, the Peacemakers sliding from their holsters as he palmed them. Jed moved up beside him, his face grim.

'They've got this side covered too, Bart,' he whispered. 'How are we going to git close enough to use our guns. They're using rifles.'

Bart cast about him swiftly, then motioned towards the cookshack. 'Over there,' he muttered tightly. 'It's our only chance. If we can make the shelter of the cookshack, we might be able to draw their fire while the others move up into position.'

He fired at the house, guns alternately pumping and bucking up and down. For a moment, the firing from the ranch slackened and he lunged forward, diving for the cookshack. He reached it and lay still for a moment, pulling air down into his heaving lungs. A smashing volley crashed out from the ranch, but the slugs either hummed harmlessly by over his head or smashed themselves against the cookshack wall and ricocheted into the distance with a whine of tortured metal. Carefully, he twisted and lifted himself on to his elbows. Window glass smashed as he fired steadily and slowly at the house. Jed had thrown himself down at the other end of the cookshack and his bullets were finding their targets as he placed his shots with effective precision. For a long moment, the answering fire died down, the Lazy V rannies finding it too dangerous to go too close to the windows.

Swiftly, Bart crammed fresh shells into the chambers. He came back into the fire just as Jed hurled his last shot at the windows. Carefully, he lifted his head until he was able to look around the edge of the shack. In the distance, he could see the troopers snaking forward through the grass, throwing lead as they advanced. There was a sudden blasting roar of sound as the whole of the Captain's force came into the battle. This was what Bart had been waiting for. Waving his right arm, he motioned the rest of the Circle W men forward. They broke free of cover and ran towards the ranch. There were a few ragged shots from the windows and one man fell, clawing at the earth in his death throes, but the others continued to race forward, scorning the lead that buzzed around them. Bart reached the wall to one side of the window, checked the chambers of his sixes, filled them quickly with slugs from his belt, then circled the ranch with the others close on his heels. A slug from one of the windows at the rear of the ranch laid a red-hot bar along his arm as he ran forward. Then Jed was pumping shots into the window from the opposite direction and a man suddenly crashed through the opening, blood on his shirt.

Kicking open the door Bart went inside. There was a tensed feeling in his body like that of a coiled spring waiting to unwind. A narrow hall led back to a winding stair. Shots came from the top of the stairs and Bart pressed himself savagely back against the wall. He heard the sound of running feet on the stairs and two men came roaring towards him, guns in their clawed hands, spitting flame as they ran.

He fired instinctively, saw one of the men fall, clutching at his chest. The other man stumbled over his body, went down on to his face, pulling up his guns as he fell. The slugs whined over Bart's shoulder and embedded themselves in the wall behind him. Jed fired in the same instant and the man's eyes glazed as his head slumped forward. His guns slithered from nerveless fingers.

Swiftly, Bart ran up the stairs, reached the top in a couple of strides and looked about him. He had the feeling that Saunders was here somewhere, that he would not risk his precious skin down below with the rest of his men, where death flew in at every window on leaden wings. No, he would be up here, probably getting together everything he could lay his heads on, hoping to escape in the confusion. Bart checked the first room. It was empty and he passed on quickly towards the second. The door was slightly ajar and some hidden instinct warned him that Saunders was standing at the back of that door with a gun in his hand, waiting for him to go in. The conviction was so strong that he knew he could not ignore it.

Carefully, silently, he padded forward, aware of the

intense sound of firing down below. Then he stepped forward swiftly and lunged heavily at the door, hurling his left shoulder at the solid woodwork. The force of the impact hurled Saunders halfway across the room. He half-fell to his knees then pushed himself upright in a single heaving motion, the guns in his hands, which he had somehow kept a tight grip on when he fell, lining up their barrels on Bart's chest.

To Bart, it was as if time had stood still. He saw the man in front of him, eyes wide and staring, filled with a blend of hatred and defeat, with fear written on his heavy features too. The other seemed to bring up his guns so slowly that even though there was a savage, desperate urgency in his movements and every line of his body, there seemed to be all the time in the world for Bart to line up his guns and squeeze the triggers. The sixes bucked in his hands and Bart saw the other's body jerk and shudder as the slugs tore into his chest, cutting into his heart. Saunders went backwards under the shattering impact, arms spread wide, the guns slipping from his fingers. There had been no chance for him to fire his guns and Bart knew that for him, the chance would never come again. The empire he had tried to build, erected on fear and terror and corruption had suddenly come to an end, toppling in pieces around him. Standing there, in that room, with Saunders lying dead on the floor in front of him, Bart felt as if all of the hate and tension had been washed clear of his body and mind. He holstered his guns, knowing by some instinct that he would not need them any more.

Going down the stairs, he found that the gun battle was over. Those of Saunders' gunmen who were still alive, had surrendered when the troopers and Circle W men had broken through into the house. Now that Saunders was dead, there was nothing left for them to fight for.

'I guess that about winds it up, Bart,' said the captain as they went outside. 'There'll be a new administration set up in Nashville very soon. Until then, the military will keep law and order. All this place needs is a chance to grow up without men like Saunders and that crooked sheriff of his around.'

'It still seems a pity that a lot of good men had to die before this could happen,' remarked Bart drily. 'Joel Benson, for example. He was a good man who tried to stand up to Saunders.'

The captain smiled. 'I reckon his daughter will still carry on the tradition,' he said quietly. 'Just what are your plans now that it's all over?'

Bart shrugged. 'I guess I'll be moving out. There's no point in me staying around here much longer. Once we turn the place over to a decent and law-abiding sheriff, I guess that's my job finished.'

'Is it?' The other looked at him curiously from beneath heavy brows. There was a twinkle in the clear grey eyes. 'if you'd asked me, I'd said that Reva Benson would need a man around the ranch now that her father's gone.'

Bart looked at the other in surprise. 'I'm a lawman, Captain, not a cattle man. I know nothin' about raisin' beef.'

The other shrugged. 'I guessed that too. But I understand that there's a job waitin' for you here if you'll take it. A lawman's job.'

For a long moment, Bart stared at the other in silence, trying to read the expression in the captain's eyes.

'I've had a word with the Marshal. He agrees with me that you'd make the best possible sheriff for Nashville. Somehow, I reckon it might be a permanent commission for you, Bart.' He held out his hand to the other as they reached the split in the trail. 'In the meantime, think over what I said about Reva Benson, won't you.'

Bart grinned, sat his saddle easily as he watched the captain and the troopers ride into Nashville. Very soon, they were out of sight along the trail. Slowly, Bart turned his horse's head into the trail which led westwards. The weariness was gone from him now as he rode with the wind in his face, back to the Circle W ranch.